Penguin Modern Classics

Homo Faber

Max Frisch, the son of an architect, was born in Zürich in 1911.
In 1933 he was forced by economic circumstances to abandon the
study of German literature at Zürich University and became a
journalist. Renewing his education, he became a trained
architect in 1943, but before this he had written his first
published work, *Leaves from a Knapsack* (1942), while doing
service with the Swiss Frontier Guard. In 1952 Frisch spent a
year in the United States and Mexico on a grant from the
Rockefeller Foundation. In 1958 he became the first foreigner to
be awarded the Büchner Prize of the German Academy for
Language and Poetry.

He has become famous outside German-speaking Europe, mainly
for his two novels *I'm Not Stiller*, also published in Penguin
Modern Classics, and *Homo Faber*.

Homo Faber

A Report by Max Frisch

Translated from the German
by Michael Bullock

Penguin Books

in association with Eyre Methuen

Penguin Books Ltd, Harmondsworth, Middlesex, England
Penguin Books, 625 Madison Avenue, New York, New York 10022, U.S.A.
Penguin Books Australia Ltd, Ringwood, Victoria, Australia
Penguin Books Canada Ltd, 2801 John Street, Markham, Ontario, Canada L3R 1B4
Penguin Books (N.Z.) Ltd, 182-190 Wairau Road, Auckland 10, New Zealand

Original German edition first published in 1957
English translation by Michael Bullock first published in
Great Britain by Abelard-Schuman 1959
This edition published by Eyre Methuen 1974
Published in Penguin Books 1974
Reprinted in Penguin Modern Classics 1983

Made and printed in Singapore by
Richard Clay (S.E.Asia) Pte Ltd.
Set in Linotype Juliana

Contents

First Stop

We were leaving from La Guardia Airport, New York, three hours late because of snow storms. Our plane, as usual on this route, was a Super Constellation. Since it was night, I immediately prepared to go to sleep. We spent another forty minutes waiting on the runway with snow in front of the searchlights, powdery snow whirling over the runway, and what made me tense and anxious, so that I couldn't get off to sleep straight away, was not the newspaper brought around by our air hostess, FIRST PICTURES OF WORLD'S GREATEST AIR CRASH IN NEVADA, a piece of news I had already seen at midday, but simply and solely the vibration in this stationary plane with its engines running – and also the young German next to me, who immediately caught my attention, I don't know why, he caught my attention the moment he took off his overcoat, when he sat down and pulled at his trouser creases, when he did nothing at all, but simply waited for the take-off like the rest of us, merely sat in his seat, a fair-haired fellow with pink skin who at once introduced himself, before we had even fastened our safety belts. I didn't catch his name, the engines were roaring, being revved up one after the other . . .

I was dead tired.

Ivy had talked away at me for three hours while we waited for the overdue plane, although she knew I was dead set against marrying.

I was glad to be alone.

At last we started.

I had never taken off in such a snow storm before: no sooner was our undercarriage off the white runway than there was nothing more to be seen of the yellow ground lights, not a glimmer, and a little later there was not a glimmer of Manhattan, it was snowing so hard. I could see only the flashing green light on our wing, which was swaying violently and occasionally jerked up and down; for seconds at a time even this flashing green light vanished in the mist and I felt like a blind man.

Permission to smoke.

He came from Düsseldorf, my neighbour, and he wasn't as young as all that, in his early thirties, younger than I at any rate; he was going to Guatemala; on business as he immediately told me . . .

The wind was buffeting the plane pretty hard.

He offered me cigarettes, my neighbour, but I took one of my own, although I had no wish to smoke, and thanked him; then I picked up the paper again; there was no desire on my part to get better acquainted. Perhaps it was rude of me. I had a hard week behind me, not a day without a conference, I wanted to rest. People are tiring. Later on, I took my papers out of my briefcase in order to work; unfortunately hot soup came along just then, and after this there was no stopping the German. (He spotted me as Swiss the moment I replied in German to his halting English.) He discussed the weather or more exactly radar, which he knew very little about. Then, as is customary since the Second World War, he began to talk about European brotherhood. I didn't say much. When we had drunk our soup I looked out of the window, although there was nothing to be seen but the flashing green light on our wet wing, the usual shower of sparks and the red glow in the engine cowl. We were still rising.

Later I slept.

The gusts of wind fell off.

I don't know why he got on my nerves, there was something familiar about his face, a very German face. I thought about it with my eyes closed, but in vain. I tried to forget his pink face, which I succeeded in doing, and slept for about six hours, worn out as I was. But no sooner was I awake than he began to get on my nerves again.

He was already eating his breakfast.

I pretended to be still asleep.

As I could see out of my right eye, we were somewhere over the Mississippi, flying at a great height and absolutely smoothly, our propellers flashing in the morning sun; the usual window-panes, you see them and at the same time look through them; the wings also glistening, rigid in empty space, no swaying now, we were poised motionless in a cloudless sky, a flight like hundreds of others; the engines running smoothly.

'Good morning,' he said.

I returned his greeting.

'Did you sleep well?' he inquired.

We could make out the tributaries of the Mississippi, though only through mist, like trickles of molten brass or bronze. It was still early in the morning, I knew this part of the run, I shut my eyes with the intention of going to sleep again.

He was reading a paperback.

It was no use shutting my eyes, I was awake and there was nothing I could do about it; I kept thinking about my neighbour, I could see him, so to speak, with my eyes shut. I ordered breakfast. . . . This was his first visit to the States, as I had supposed, but his opinion of the country was already cut and dried; on the whole, he found the Americans lacking in culture, but there were certain things of which he could not help approving, for instance the friendly attitude of most Americans towards Germany.

I didn't contradict.

No German wanted rearmament, but the Russians were

forcing it on America, it was tragic, as a Swiss (a Switzer, he called it) I couldn't judge these things because I'd never been in the Caucasus, he had been in the Caucasus, he knew Ivan and you could only teach him with weapons. He knew Ivan! He repeated this several times. You could only teach him with weapons, he said. Nothing else made any impression on Ivan ...

I peeled my apple.

To distinguish between the master races and inferior races, as Hitler did, was nonsense of course; but Asiatics were always Asiatics ...

I ate my apple.

I took my electric shaver out of my briefcase in order to shave or rather to be alone for a quarter of an hour; I don't like Germans, although my friend Joachim was also a German. ... In the washroom I wondered whether I should move to another seat. I just didn't feel like getting better acquainted with this gentleman, and it would be at least another four hours before we reached Mexico City, where my neighbour had to change planes. I had made up my mind to sit somewhere else; there were a number of places free. When I came back into the cabin, shaved, so that I felt freer, more confident – I can't bear being unshaven – he had just taken the liberty of picking up my papers from the floor in case somebody trod on them. He handed them to me, politeness personified. I thanked him as I stowed the papers away in my briefcase, rather too cordially, it seems, since he immediately took advantage of my thanks to ask more questions.

Did I work for UNESCO?

I felt my stomach – as I often did recently. There was no real pain, I was simply aware of having a stomach, a stupid feeling. Perhaps that was why I was so disagreeable. I sat down in my old seat and in order not to be disagreeable, told him I was concerned in TECHNICAL AID TO UNDER-

DEVELOPED COUNTRIES; I can talk about this while thinking of something entirely different. I don't know what I was thinking about. He seemed to be impressed by UNESCO, as he was by anything international, he stopped treating me as a 'Switzer' and listened as though I were an authority, with positive reverence, interested to the point of subservience, which didn't prevent him from getting on my nerves.

I was glad when we landed.

Just as we left the plane and parted in front of the customs shed I realized what it was that had struck me earlier; his face, though plump and pink as Joachim's never was, none the less reminded me of Joachim . . .

Then I forgot it.

That was in Houston, Texas.

After the customs, after the usual palaver about my camera, which has been half way round the world with me, I went into the bar for a drink, but noticed that my Düsseldorfer was already sitting in the bar and actually keeping a stool free – presumably for me! – and went straight down into the washroom, where, having nothing else to do, I washed my hands.

We were stopping twenty minutes.

As I first washed and then dried my hands, I saw my face in the mirror, as white as wax with patches of grey and yellow and purple veins, a horrible sight, like the face of a corpse. I assumed it was due to the neon light and dried my hands, which were also yellowish-purple; then came the usual announcement over the loudspeaker, which was transmitted to every part of the building, consequently also to the basement. ATTENTION PLEASE, ATTENTION PLEASE. I didn't know what was happening. My hands were sweating; although it was positively cold in this washroom, it was hot outside. All I knew was that when I came to a fat coloured woman was bending over me, a cleaner whom I hadn't no-

13

ticed before; she was only a few inches away, I could see her enormous mouth with the black lips and her pink gums; I heard the echoing loudspeaker while I was still on my hands and knees.

THE PLANE IS READY FOR DEPARTURE.

And again:

THE PLANE IS READY FOR DEPARTURE.

I was used to this public address system.

ALL PASSENGERS FOR MEXICO – GUATEMALA – PANAMA, in between engines roaring, KINDLY REQUESTED, engines roaring, GATE NUMBER FIVE, THANK YOU.

I stood up.

The coloured woman was still kneeling.

I swore never to smoke again and tried to hold my face under the tap, but couldn't because of the basin. It was a sweating attack, that was all, a sweating attack accompanied by dizziness.

ATTENTION PLEASE.

I felt better at once.

PASSENGER FABER, PASSENGER FABER.

That was I.

PLEASE CALL AT THE INFORMATION DESK.

I heard the message, I dipped my face in the basin, I hoped they would fly on without me, the water was very little colder than my sweat, I couldn't understand why the coloured woman suddenly burst out laughing – it made her breasts shake like jelly; that was how she had to laugh with her enormous mouth, her frizzy hair, her white and black eyes, a close-up from Africa. Then it came again: THE PLANE IS READY FOR DEPARTURE. I dried my face with a handkerchief, while the coloured woman brushed my trousers. I even combed my hair merely to waste time, announcement after announcement came over the loudspeaker, arrivals, departures, then once again:

14

She refused to accept money, it was a pleasure for her that I was still alive, that the Lord had heard her prayer. I just put the bank note down beside her, but she followed me out on to the stairs where, as a Negro, she wasn't allowed to go, and forced the note into my hand.

The bar was empty.

I slipped on to a stool, lit a cigarette, watched the barman drop the usual olive into the cold glass and then pour the liquid on to it with the usual movement, holding the strainer in front of the silver cocktail shaker with his thumb, so that no ice should drop into the glass, and I put my bank note down; outside, a Super-Constellation rolled past and out on to the runway for the take-off. Without me! I was drinking my dry martini when the loudspeaker began to rumble again. ATTENTION PLEASE. For a while there was nothing to be heard, the engines of the departing Super-Constellation were roaring just outside before it rose into the air and flew off over our heads. Then again:

PASSENGER FABER, PASSENGER FABER . . .

Nobody could know this referred to me, and I told myself they couldn't wait much longer. I went up on to the observation roof to see our plane. It was standing there looking as though it was ready to take off: the Shell tankers had gone, but the propellers weren't turning. I drew a deep breath as I saw our passengers streaming across the empty airfield to go aboard, my Düsseldorfer near the front. I waited for the propellers to start turning, the loudspeaker echoed and crackled here too.

PLEASE GO TO THE INFORMATION DESK.

But it wasn't for me.

MISS SHERBON, MR AND MRS ROSENTHAL . . .

I waited and waited, the four crosses of the propellers remained absolutely still. I couldn't stand this feeling of being waited for, and went down into the basement again, where I

hid behind the bolted door of a toilet. Then it came again:
PASSENGER FABER, PASSENGER FABER.

It was a woman's voice. And I was sweating again and had to sit down to save myself from feeling giddy. My feet were visible.

THIS IS OUR LAST CALL.

Again: THIS IS OUR LAST CALL.

I don't really know why I was hiding. I was ashamed of myself; I'm not generally the last. I stayed in my hiding place at least ten minutes after the loudspeaker had given me up. I simply didn't feel like flying any farther. I waited behind the bolted door until I heard the thunder of an engine taking off, a Super-Constellation. I know the sound! Then I rubbed my face, so that my pallor shouldn't attract attention, and left the toilet like any ordinary person. I whistled to myself, I stood in the hall and bought some newspaper or other, I had no idea what to do in this Houston, Texas. It was strange: suddenly everything was happening without me. I listened every time the loudspeaker boomed – then, for the sake of something to do, I walked over to the Western Union counter to send a cable about my luggage, which was flying on to Mexico without me, then a cable to Caracas saying that the assembly of the turbines should be postponed twenty-four hours, then a cable to New York. I was just putting my ballpoint pen back in my pocket, when our air hostess, the usual list in her other hand, took me by the elbow.

'There you are!'

I was speechless.

'We're late, Mr Faber, we're late.'

I followed her holding my superfluous cables, with all sorts of excuses that were of no interest, out to our Super-Constellation; I walked like a man being led out of jail into the court room – my eyes on the floor or on the gangway, which was detached and wheeled away the moment I was inside the cabin.

'I'm sorry,' I said, 'I'm sorry.'

The passengers, their safety belts already fastened, turned to look at me without a word, and my Düsseldorfer, whom I had forgotten, immediately gave me back my window seat. He was very concerned as to what had happened. I told him my watch had stopped and took it off my wrist.

Take-off normal.

The next thing my neighbour told me was interesting – I found him altogether more congenial now that my stomach was no longer troubling me. He admitted that the German cigar was not yet among the world's best, the first essential for a good cigar, he said, was good tobacco.

He unfolded a map.

The plantation his firm hoped to develop lay, it seemed, at the end of the world, territory of Guatemala, to be reached from Flores only on horseback, whereas from Palenque (territory of Mexico) you could get to it by jeep without trouble; even a Nash, he asserted, had been driven through this jungle.

He himself was flying there for the first time.

Population: Indians.

It interested me, inasmuch as I, too, was concerned with the exploitation of underdeveloped areas; we agreed that roads would have to be built, perhaps even a small airfield, it was all a question of connections, the goods would be shipped at Puerto Barrios. A bold enterprise, it seemed to me, not unreasonable, however, perhaps really the future of the German cigar.

He folded up the map.

I wished him good luck.

You couldn't see anything on his map (1:500,000) anyway, a no man's land, white with two blue lines, rivers, between green state frontiers, the only names (in red and unreadable without a magnifying glass) referred to Maya ruins.

I wished him good luck.

A brother of his, who had been living there for months, was obviously having trouble with the climate – I could just imagine it, flat, tropical country, the humidity during the rainy reason, the vertical sun.

That was the end of the conversation.

I smoked, gazing out of the window: below, the Gulf of Mexico, a multitude of little clouds casting violet shadows on the greenish sea, the usual play of colours, I had filmed it often enough. I shut my eyes to catch up on some of the sleep Ivy had robbed me of. The aeroplane was now absolutely quiet; so was my neighbour.

He was reading his novel.

Novels don't interest me. Nor do dreams. I dreamed about Ivy, I think, anyhow I felt oppressed, it was in a Las Vegas poolroom (I've never been to Las Vegas in reality), there was a tremendous din and above it loudspeakers kept calling out my name, a chaos of blue and red and yellow automatic machines at which you could win money, a lottery, I was waiting among a lot of stark naked people to be divorced (though in reality I'm not married), somehow Professor O., my esteemed teacher at the Swiss College of Technology, was in it, he was wildly sentimental and kept weeping all the time, although he is a mathematician, or rather a professor of electrodynamics, it was very embarrassing, but the craziest thing of all, I was married to the Düsseldorfer! ... I wanted to protest, but couldn't open my mouth without holding my hand over it, for all my teeth had just fallen out, I could feel them in my mouth like so many pebbles ...

The moment I woke up I knew what was happening.

Beneath us the open sea ...

It was the left-hand engine that had broken down; one propeller stood out like a rigid cross against the cloudless sky – that was all.

Beneath us, as I have said, the Gulf of Mexico.

Our air hostess, a girl of twenty, little more than a child to look at had taken hold of my left shoulder to wake me, but I realized what was going on before she told me, handing me a green life-jacket as she spoke; my neighbour was in the act of fastening his life-jacket, jokingly as in all such emergency drills.

We were flying at an altitude of at least six thousand feet.

Of course none of my teeth had fallen out, not even my crowned tooth, right upper fourth; I felt relieved, positively cheerful.

From the corridor in front the captain announced:

THERE IS NO DANGER WHATEVER.

The life-jackets were just a precaution, our plane could have gone on flying even with two engines, we were eight and a half miles from the Mexican coast, heading for Tampico, all passengers were kindly requested to keep calm and for the moment not to smoke.

THANK YOU.

Everyone sat as though in church, all with green life-jackets on their chests. I explored with my tongue to make sure that none of my teeth were really loose, nothing else worried me.

Time: 10.25 a.m.

If we hadn't been delayed by the snowstorm in the northern United States we should have landed in Mexico by now. I said so to my Düsseldorfer, merely for the sake of talking. I hate solemnity.

No reply.

I asked him what time he had.

No reply.

The engines, the other three, were running smoothly, and there was nothing to suggest any of these might cut out, we were not losing height, I could see that; then the coast in a haze, a kind of lagoon, beyond it swamps. No trace of Tampico yet, however. I remembered Tampico from an earlier visit, from a fish-poisoning I shall never forget as long as I live.

'Tampico,' I said, 'that's the filthiest town in the world, an oil port, you'll see, it stinks either of oil or of fish . . .'

He was fingering his life-jacket.

'I'll give you a piece of advice,' I said. 'Don't eat any fish, whatever you do . . .'

He tried to smile.

'The natives are immune, of course,' I said, 'but it's different for us . . .'

He nodded, without hearing. It seems I delivered quite a lecture on amoebas and on Tampico hotels. As soon as I noticed my Düsseldorfer wasn't listening, I took him by the sleeve, a thing I don't normally do, on the contrary, I hate this mania for taking hold of people's sleeves. But otherwise he just wouldn't have listened. I told him the whole tedious story of my ptomaine poisoning in Tampico in 1951, that is to say six years ago. Then I noticed that we were not flying parallel with the coast, but had turned inland. So we weren't making for Tampico. I was amazed, and wanted to ask the air hostess what was going on.

Permission to smoke again.

Perhaps the Tampico airport was too small for our Super-Constellation (the other time it was a DC-4), or they had received instructions to fly on to Mexico City in spite of the engine trouble, which I couldn't understand, with the Sierra Madre Oriental still in front of us. Our air hostess – I caught her elbow, a thing, as I have said, which I don't normally do – had no time to answer questions, she had been called to the pilot.

We were actually gaining height.

I tried to think of Ivy.

We were gaining height.

Beneath us there were still swamps, shallow and turbid,

divided by tongues of land, sand, the swamps were green in some places and in others red, the red of a lipstick, something I couldn't understand, they were really not swamps but lagoons, and where they reflected the sun they glittered like tinsel or tinfoil, anyhow with a metallic glint, then again they were sky-blue and watery (like Ivy's eyes) with yellow shoals and patches like violet ink, sombre, probably due to underwater plants, at one point a river flowed into the swamp, brown like milky American coffee, it was repulsive, nothing but lagoons mile after mile. The Düsseldorfer also had the feeling we were gaining height.

People were talking again.

There wasn't even a decent map here, such as SWISSAIR always has available; and what got on my nerves was the idiotic information that the plane was making for Tampico, when it was really heading inland – and gaining height, as I have said, with three engines; I watched the three glittering discs, which occasionally seem to hesitate, though this is only an optical illusion, they were still the usual rotating circles of black. There was no cause for alarm. It was just that the rigid cross of a stationary propeller looks odd when you are in full flight.

I felt sorry for our air hostess.

She had to go from one row of seats to the next with an advertisement smile, asking if everybody felt comfortable in his life-jacket; as soon as someone made a little joke, she stopped smiling. 'Can you swim in the mountains?' I asked her.

Orders were orders.

I held the young lady, who could have been my daughter, by the arm, or rather by the wrist, and told her (jokingly, of course), shaking my finger at her, that she and she alone had forced me to make this flight. She answered:

'There's no danger, sir, no danger at all. We're going

to land in Mexico City in about an hour and twenty minutes.'

That's what she told everyone.

I let her go, so that she could smile again and do her job, making sure everybody was fastened in. Shortly after this she received orders to bring lunch round, although it wasn't lunch-time yet. . . . Fortunately the weather was fine overland too, almost no clouds, though there were gusts of wind as usual before mountains, the normal thermic conditions, so that our plane dropped and shook until it recovered its balance and started to gain height again, before dropping once more with its wings rocking; for minutes at a time we flew along perfectly smoothly, then there came another bump that set the wings vibrating and the whole plane rolling again, until it righted itself once more and gained fresh height, as though it had straightened itself out for good now, till the next bump – the usual thing in turbulent air.

In the distance the blue mountains.

Sierra Madre Oriental.

Below us the red desert.

Shortly after this – my Düsseldorfer and I had just been given our lunch, the usual thing, fruit juice and a white sandwich with green salad – a second engine suddenly cut out, there was the inevitable panic, in spite of the lunch everybody had on his knees. Someone yelled.

From this moment on everything moved very fast.

The captain had obviously decided to make a forced landing, for fear the remaining engines might cut out. At all events we were losing height; the loudspeaker crackled and spluttered, so that we could scarcely understand a word of the instructions we were being given.

My first worry: what to do with the lunch.

We were losing height, although, as I said, two engines should have been enough; the landing wheels were out, as usual before a landing, and I simply put my lunch tray down on the floor in the gangway, although we were still at least fifteen hundred feet up.

The air turbulence had stopped.

NO SMOKING.

I was aware of the danger that our plane might break in pieces or go up in flames as it landed – I was astounded at my own calm.

I didn't think of anyone.

Things happened very quickly, as I have said; beneath us sand, a shallow valley between hills that seemed to be rocky, bare desert all around.

Actually I felt only curious.

We were coming in to land exactly as though there was an airstrip underneath us; I pressed my face to the window, you never see the runway till the last minute, when the brake-flaps are already out. I was surprised that the brake-flaps didn't appear. Our plane was obviously avoiding any curve so as not to lose height and we flew on over the flat inviting plain; our shadow moved closer and closer to us, flying faster than we, so it seemed, a grey rag on the reddish sand, flapping.

Then rocks.

We rose again.

Then, fortunately, sand again, but sand interspersed with agaves; we flew for some minutes at house-height, both engines at full speed, the undercarriage retracted again. That meant a belly landing. We were flying as one otherwise flies only at great heights, rather quietly and without an under-carriage – but at house-height, as I have said, and I knew there was no runway coming, nevertheless I pressed my face to the window.

Our undercarriage was suddenly lowered again, although there was no runway coming, and also the brake-flaps; you felt it like a punch in the stomach, brakes, a drop as though in a lift; at the last moment I lost my nerve, so that the landing – all I saw were the agaves racing past on either side, then both hands over my face – was nothing but a blind bump, a crashing forward into unconsciousness.

Then silence.

We were damn lucky, I must say, nobody had so much as opened an emergency exit, I hadn't myself, nobody moved, we hung forward, suspended on our safety belts.

'Go on,' said the captain, 'go on.'

No one moved.

'Go on.'

Fortunately there was no fire. People had to be told they could unfasten their belts, the doors were open, but of course no steps were wheeled up, the way we were used to, nothing but heat, like the air that comes out of an oven when you open the door, burning hot.

I was uninjured.

Finally the rope ladder.

Without waiting for an order we all gathered in the shade under the wing; not a word was spoken, as though talking in the desert was forbidden. Our Super-Constellation was tilted slightly forward, there was no serious damage, only the front undercarriage was jammed, having sunk into the sand, it wasn't even smashed up. The four propeller-crosses gleamed in the glaring blue sky; so did the three rudders. No one moved, as I said; obviously everyone was waiting for the captain to say something.

'Well,' he said, 'here we are.'

He laughed.

All around nothing but agaves, sand, the reddish mountains in the distance, farther off than I had previously estimated, but above all sand and again sand, yellow, with the shimmer of hot air over it, like molten glass.

Time: 11.05 a.m.

I wound up my watch.

The crew brought out blankets to protect the rubber tyres from the sun, while we stood around in our green life-jackets doing nothing. I don't know why no one took his life-jacket off.

*

I don't believe in providence and fate, as a technologist I am used to reckoning with the formulae of probability. What has providence to do with it? I admit that without this forced landing in Tamaulipas (? April) everything would have turned out differently: I should never have got to know this young Hencke, I should perhaps never have heard of Hanna again, I shouldn't know today that I was a father. It is impossible to imagine what would have happened if it hadn't been for this forced landing in Tamaulipas. Sabeth might still be alive. I don't deny that it was more than a coincidence which made things turn out as they did, it was a whole train of coincidences. But what has providence to do with it? I don't need any mystical explanation for the occurrence of the improbable; mathematics explains it adequately, as far as I'm concerned.

Mathematically speaking, the probable (that in 6,000,000,000 throws with a regular six-sided die the one will come up approximately 1,000,000,000 times) and the improbable (that in six throws with the same die the one will come up six times) are not different in kind, but only in frequency, whereby the more frequent appears *a priori* more probable. But the occasional occurrence of the improbable does not imply the intervention of a higher power, something in the nature of a miracle, as the layman is so ready to assume. The term probability includes improbability at the extreme limits of probability, and when the improbable does occur this is no cause for surprise, bewilderment or mystification.

Cf. Ernst Mally's *Probability and Law*, Hans Reichenbach's *The Theory of Probability*, Whitehead and Russell's *Principia*

*

We remained in the desert of Tamaulipas, Mexico, for four days and three nights, eighty-five hours in all, and there is little to report of this stay. It was not a magnificent experience, as everybody seems to expect when I talk about it. It was much too hot for that! Naturally I thought straight away of the Disney film, which was magnificent, and got out my camera; but absolutely nothing sensational happened, just an occasional lizard, which made me jump, and some creatures like sand spiders, that was all.

There was nothing to do but wait.

The first thing I did in the desert of Tamaulipas was to introduce myself to the Düsseldorfer, because he was interested in my camera; I explained its optics to him.

Other people were reading.

Fortunately, it soon turned out that he played chess, and as I always take my pocket chess set with me when I'm travelling, we were saved; he immediately organized a couple of empty Coca-Cola crates, we sat down away from the rest to escape from the general chatter, in the shadow of the tail-plane – with nothing on but shoes (because of the hot sand) and jockey shorts.

The afternoon passed in no time.

Shortly before dusk, an aircraft appeared, a military plane, circled for a long time overhead without dropping anything, and disappeared (I filmed this) northwards, in the direction of Monterrey.

Supper: a cheese sandwich, half a banana.

I like chess because you can spend hours at a time without speaking. You don't even have to listen when your opponent talks. You stare at the board and it isn't in the least rude if you show no desire for personal contact, but devote all your attention to the game.

'It's your move,' he said.

The discovery that he not only knew my friend Joachim, from whom I hadn't heard a word for twenty years, but was actually his brother, came by chance. ... When the moon rose (I also filmed this) between black agaves on the horizon, we could have gone on playing chess, it was so light, but suddenly too cold; we trudged out to smoke a cigarette, out into the sand, where I admitted that landscapes didn't mean much to me, and certainly not a desert.

'You don't mean that!' he said.

He thought it experience.

'Let's turn in,' I said. 'Hotel Super-Constellation, a holiday in the desert with all modern convenience.'

I felt cold.

I've often wondered what people mean when they talk about an experience. I'm a technologist and accustomed to seeing things as they are. I see everything they are talking about very clearly; after all, I'm not blind. I see the moon over the Tamaulipas desert – it is more distinct than at other times, perhaps, but still a calculable mass circling round our planet, an example of gravitation, interesting, but in what way an experience? I see the jagged rocks, standing out black against the moonlight; perhaps they do look like the jagged backs of prehistoric monsters, but I know they are rocks, stone, probably volcanic, one would have to examine them to be sure of this. Why should I feel afraid? There aren't any prehistoric monsters any more. Why should I imagine them? I'm sorry, but I don't see any stone angels either; nor demons; I see what I see – the usual shapes due to erosion and also my long shadow on the sand, but no ghosts. Why get womanish? I don't see any Flood either, but sand lit up by the moon and made undulating, like water, by the wind, which doesn't surprise me; I don't find it fantastic, but perfectly explicable. I don't know what the souls of the damned looked like; perhaps like black agaves in the desert at night. What I see are agaves, a plant that blossoms once only and then dies. Furthermore, I know (however it may look at the moment) that I am not the last or the first man on earth; and I can't be moved by the mere idea that I am the last man, because it isn't true. Why get hysterical? Mountains are mountains, even if in a certain light they may look like something else, but it is the Sierra Madre Oriental, and we are not standing in a kingdom of the dead, but in the Tamaulipas desert, Mexico, about sixty miles from the nearest road, which is unpleasant, but in what way an experience? An aeroplane to me is an aeroplane, I can't see it as a dead bird, it is a Super-Constellation with engine trouble, nothing more, and it makes no difference how much the moon shines on it. Why should I experience what isn't there? Nor can I bring myself to hear something resembling eternity; I don't hear anything, apart from the trickle of sand at every step. I am shivering, but I know that in seven to eight hours the sun will be shining again. What is all this about the end of the world? I can't imagine a lot of nonsense, merely in order to experience something. I see the sandy horizon, whitish in the green light, twenty miles away at a guess, and I don't see why there, in the direction of Tampico, the Other World should begin. I know Tampico. I refuse to feel afraid simply because of an over-active imagination, or to start imagining things simply because I feel afraid. It was altogether too mystical for me.

'Come on,' I said.

Herbert stood there, still experiencing.

'By the way,' I said, 'are you any relation of a Joachim Hencke, who once studied in Zurich?'

It just slipped out as we stood there, our hands in our pockets and our coat-collars turned up; we were on the point of climbing up into the cabin.

'Joachim?' he said. 'That's my brother.'

'No!' I said.

'Yes,' he said, 'of course – I told you I was going to visit my brother in Guatemala.'

We had to laugh.

'It's a small world!'

We spent the nights in the cabin, shivering in an overcoat and rugs; the crew made tea, as long as the water lasted.

'How is he?' I inquired. 'I haven't heard anything of him for twenty years.'

'He's all right,' replied Herbert, 'he's all right . . .'

'We were very good friends in those days,' I said.

What I heard was the usual story: marriage, a child (which I didn't quite catch, obviously, otherwise I shouldn't have asked again later on), then the war, a prison camp, return to Düsseldorf and so on; it shook me to think how time passes, how we grow older.

'We're worried,' he said.

'Why?'

'He's the only white man down there,' he said, 'and we've had no news for two months.'

He told me about it.

Most of the passengers were already asleep, we had to whisper, the main light in the cabin had been turned off long ago, and, to save current, we had been asked to switch off the little lights over the seats; it was dark; only the brightness of the sand outside, the wings in the moonlight, gleaming, cold.

'Why should there have been an uprising?'

I calmed him down.

'Why an uprising?' I said. 'Perhaps his letters simply went astray . . .'

Someone asked us to keep quiet.

Forty-two passengers in a Super-Constellation that wasn't flying, but standing in the desert, an aeroplane with rugs around the engines (to keep the sand out) and with rugs around every wheel, the passengers exactly as though they were flying, sleeping in their seats with their heads to one side and most of them with their mouths open, but all in deathly silence, outside the four polished propeller-crosses, the white moonlight on the wings, everything motionless – it was a funny sight.

Someone was talking in his sleep.

When I woke up in the morning, looked out of the little window and saw the sand, the nearness of the sand, I took fright for a second, unnecessarily.

Herbert was reading a paperback again.

I took out my calendar. 3 April, assemble turbines at Caracas!

For breakfast there was fruit juice with two biscuits and further assurances that food was on the way, also drinks, there was nothing to worry about. It would have been better if they had said nothing; as it was, of course, we waited all day long for the sound of engines.

Another day of maddening heat.

It was even hotter in the cabin.

All we heard was the wind, the occasional whistle of sand mice, which we didn't see, the scuffle of a lizard, and especially a perpetual wind that didn't lift the sand, but simply blew it along the ground, so that our footsteps were again and again obliterated; again and again it looked as though no one had been here, no company of forty-two passengers and five members of the crew.

I wished I could shave.

There was absolutely nothing to film.

I don't feel comfortable when unshaven; not on account of other people, but on my own account. Not being shaved gives me the feeling I'm some sort of plant and I keep involuntarily feeling my chin. I took out my shaver and tried every possible way of getting it to work. Of course it was no use: you can't use an electric razor without any electric current, I knew that

– that was what put me so much on edge, the fact that in the desert there is no current, no telephone, no power points, nothing.

Once, around noon, we heard engines.

Everyone, except Herbert and me, was standing outside in the broiling sun, watching the purple sky over the yellow sand and the grey thistles and the red mountains; it was only a thin hum, an ordinary DC-7 glittering up there at a great altitude, white as snow in the reflected light, heading for Mexico City, where we ought to have landed yesterday at about this time.

Our spirits dropped lower than ever.

Fortunately, we had our chess.

Many passengers followed our example, taking off everything but their shoes and their underpants; it was harder for the ladies, some of them sat with tucked up skirts and brassières, blue or white or pink, with their blouses wound round their heads like turbans.

A lot of people complained of headaches.

Somebody had to vomit.

Herbert and I were sitting apart from the rest again, in the shade of the tailplane, which, like the wings, was dazzling with the sunlight reflected off the sand, so that even in the shadow it was like sitting under a searchlight. As usual while playing chess, we spoke little. At one point I asked:

'Isn't Joachim married any more, then?'

'No,' he said.

'Divorced?'

'Yes,' he said.

'We used to play a lot of chess in the old days.'

'Oh,' he said.

His monosyllables irritated me.

'Who did he marry?'

I asked simply to pass the time, not being allowed to smoke made me edgy, I had an unlit cigarette in my mouth; it was

31

taking Herbert so long to make up his mind, although he must have seen his position was hopeless; I was a knight up and therefore well ahead; then, after a long silence and quite casually, as casually as I had asked my questions, he mentioned Hanna's name.

'. . . Hanna Landsberg, from Munich, half Jewish.'

I said nothing.

'It's your move,' he said.

I hid my feelings, I believe. I inadvertently lit my cigarette, which was strictly forbidden, so I quickly put it out again. I pretended to be thinking over my next move, and lost piece after piece.

'What's the matter with you?' he laughed.

We didn't finish the game, I gave up and turned the board around in order to set the men up again. I didn't even dare to ask whether Hanna was still alive. We played for hours without uttering a word, every now and then shifting our Coca-Cola crate so as to stay in the shade. This meant forever sitting down on sand that a moment ago had been baking in the sun. We were sweating as though in a Turkish bath, bent over my leather pocket chess set, which was unfortunately getting discoloured by our dripping sweat.

There was nothing left to drink.

Why I didn't ask whether Hanna was still alive, I don't know – perhaps for fear he would tell me Hanna had been sent to Theresienstadt.

I worked out her present age.

I couldn't picture her.

Towards evening, just before dusk, the promised aircraft arrived, a sports plane; it circled around for a long time before it finally ventured to drop the parachute – three sacks and two boxes that had to be collected from within a radius of three hundred yards – we were saved. CARTA BLANCA, CERVEZA MEXICANA, a good beer, even Herbert, the German, had to admit as we stood with our beer tins in the desert, a social gathering in brassières and underpants with another sunset, which I took on coloured film.

I dreamed of Hanna.

Hanna as a nurse on horseback.

On the third day the first helicopter came, to fetch at least the Argentinian mama and her two children, thank goodness, and to take mail; it waited an hour for mail.

Herbert immediately wrote to Düsseldorf.

Everyone sat writing.

You pretty well had to write, if only to stop kind people from asking whether you had no wife, no mother, no children – I took out my Baby Hermes (it's still full of sand) and slipped in a sheet of paper with a carbon copy, since I thought I was going to write to Williams. I typed the date and pushed the carriage over to begin the letter.

'My dear ...'

So I wrote to Ivy. I had long felt a desire to make a clean breast of it. At last I had time and peace, the peace of a whole desert.

'My dear ...'

It didn't take long to tell her I was sitting in the desert, sixty miles from the world of normal transport. That it was hot, fine weather, not the slightest injury and so on, and a few descriptive details to add local colour – Coca-Cola crate, underpants, meeting with a fellow chess enthusiast – all this didn't fill a letter. What else? Beer at last. What else? I couldn't even ask her to get films for me and I knew that Ivy, like every woman, really only wanted to know what I felt – or thought, if I didn't feel anything. I knew what this was, all right: I hadn't married Hanna, whom I loved, so why should I marry Ivy? But it was damned difficult to put this into words without hurting her feelings, for she didn't know anything about Hanna and was a nice kid, but the sort of American woman who thinks she has to marry every man she goes to bed with. At the same time, Ivy was thoroughly married, I didn't know how many times altogether, but her present husband, a Washington official, had no intention of getting a divorce; for he loved Ivy. I don't know whether he had any idea why Ivy regularly flew to New York. She used to say she was going to the psychiatrist, and as a matter of fact she did that too. Anyhow, no one ever knocked at my door, and I couldn't see why Ivy, who in other ways had a modern outlook, was so insistent about making a marriage of it; anyway, we had done nothing but row lately, it seemed to me, row about every little thing. We rowed about whether it should be a Studebaker or a Nash! I only had to think of it – and suddenly my fingers typed by themselves; in fact now I had to keep looking at my watch to be sure of having my letter finished by the time the helicopter took off.

Its engine was already running.

I didn't want the Studebaker, that was Ivy's idea; the colour especially (tomato-red in her opinion, raspberry-red in mine) was her taste, not mine, she wasn't much interested in the technical qualities of the car. Ivy was a model, she chose her clothes according to the colour of the car, I think, and the colour of the car according to her lipstick or the other way around, I'm not sure which it was. I only knew her eternal reproach – that I had no taste at all and that I wouldn't marry her. And yet she was a good kid, as I said. But she was horrified that I should want to sell her Studebaker and considered it typical of me that I didn't give a moment's thought to her wardrobe, for I was an egotist, a brute, a barbarian where taste was concerned, a monster as regards women. I knew her reproaches and was fed up with them. I had told her often enough that I definitely wouldn't get married, or anyhow I had made it pretty clear, and in the end I definitely told her so, it was at the airport, when we had to wait three hours for this Super-Constellation. Ivy actually cried, and therefore listened to what I was saying. But perhaps Ivy needed it in black and white. If we had been burnt to death when we made this forced landing she would have been able to live without me! I told her sufficiently plainly (fortunately with a carbon copy), so I thought, to save us from another meeting.

The helicopter was ready to take off.

I had no time to read through my letter, but only to put it in an envelope, gum it up and hand it in – and watch the helicopter take off.

We were slowly growing beards.

I longed for electric current.

The situation was gradually getting tedious, in fact it was scandalous that the forty-two passengers and five crew members should not have been liberated long ago from this desert; after all, most of us were travelling on urgent business.

In the end I did ask:

'Tell me, is she still alive?'

'Who?' he asked.

'Hanna – his wife.'

'Oh, I see,' he said and thought about the best way of countering my opening gambit, whistling all the time, which got on my nerves at the best of times, whistling under his breath without any tune, an involuntary hissing sound like an outlet valve – I had to repeat my question.

'Where does she live now?'

'Don't know,' he said.

'But she is alive still?'

'I suppose so.'

'Don't you know?'

'No,' he said. 'But I suppose so.' He repeated everything like his own echo. 'I suppose so.'

Our game of chess was more important to him.

'Perhaps it's too late anyhow,' he said later. 'Perhaps it's too late anyhow.'

He was referring to the chess.

'Did she have a chance to emigrate?'

'Yes,' he said, 'she did.'

'1938,' he said, 'at the last moment.'

'Where to?'

'Paris,' he said. 'Then probably somewhere else, for we were in Paris ourselves a few years later. I never enjoyed myself so much in my life! That was before I went to the Caucasus. *Sous les toits de Paris!*'

There wasn't much more to be got out of him.

'I think I've had it,' he said, 'unless I exchange man for man.'

We were playing with less and less enthusiasm.

As we learned later, eight U.S. Army helicopters were waiting at the Mexican frontier for permission to pick us up.

I cleaned my Baby Hermes.

Herbert read.

There was nothing to do but wait.

*

As regards Hanna:

I couldn't possibly have married Hanna; at that time – 1933 to 1935 – I was an assistant lecturer at the Swiss College of Technology, Zurich, working on my dissertation (on the significance of the so-called Maxwell's demon) and earning 300 francs a month, marriage was out of the question on economic grounds, apart from anything else. Nor did Hanna ever reproach me for not marrying her. I was quite ready to do so. It was really Hanna herself who didn't want to marry at that time.

*

My decision to change route on an official trip and make a private detour via Guatemala, merely to see an old friend of my youth again, was reached on the airfield at Mexico City and at the very last moment. I was already standing at the barrier, shaking hands all over again and asking Herbert to give his brother my best wishes, if he remembered me at all, when the usual announcement came over the loudspeaker: ATTENTION PLEASE, ATTENTION PLEASE (it was another Super-Constellation), WILL ALL PASSENGERS FOR PANAMA – CARACAS – PERNAMBUCO ... I just couldn't face the prospect of climbing into another aeroplane, fastening another safety belt. Herbert said:

'It's time you got moving.'

I am generally considered extremely conscientious over professional matters, perhaps excessively so, anyhow I have never before postponed an official trip for a passing whim, let alone changed my route. An hour later I was flying with Herbert.

'Well,' he said, 'that's sporting of you.'

I don't know what it was really.

'Now the turbines are waiting for me for a change,' I said. 'I've waited for them often enough, now they can wait for me.'

Of course, that was no way to look at it.

As soon as we reached Campeche the heat greeted us with slimy sunshine and sticky air, the stench of slime rotting in the sun, and when you wiped the sweat from your face it was as though you yourself stank of fish. I said nothing. In the end you stop wiping the sweat away and sit there with your eyes closed, breathing with your mouth shut, resting your head against a wall and sticking your legs out in front of you. Herbert was quite sure the train went every Tuesday, he had it in black and white in a Düsseldorf guidebook – but after waiting five hours we suddenly discovered it was not Tuesday, but Monday.

I didn't say a word.

At least there was a shower in the hotel, and a towel that smelled of camphor as is usual in this part of the world; when

I went to take a shower, beetles as long as my finger fell from the mouldy curtain – I tried to drown them, but they kept climbing up out of the plug-hole again, until I squashed them under my heel so that I could finally have my shower.

I dreamed of those beetles.

I had made up my mind to leave Herbert and fly back the following afternoon, friendship or no friendship ...

I felt my stomach again.

I was lying stark naked.

It stank all night long.

Herbert also lay stark naked.

In spite of everything, Campeche is a town, a human settlement with electric current so that you can shave, and telephones; but there were zopilotes perched on every wire, waiting in rows for a dog to die of hunger, a donkey to collapse, a horse to be slaughtered, then they would come flapping down ... We arrived just as they were tugging a long tangle of entrails this way and that, a whole pack of blackish-purple birds with bloody guts in their beaks, they wouldn't fly away, even when a car came along; they dragged the carcass off somewhere else, without rising into the air, just hopping and scurrying, and all this right in the middle of the market place.

Herbert bought a pineapple.

As I said, I had made up my mind to fly back to Mexico City. I was in despair. I have no idea why I didn't do so.

Suddenly it was midday.

We were standing outside on an embankment, where it stank less but was even hotter, because there was no shade, eating our pineapple; we leaned forward because of the dripping juice, then we bent down over the stones and rinsed our sugary fingers; the warm water was also sticky, not sugary but salty, and our fingers smelled of seaweed, of motor oil, of shells, of unidentifiable rotting matter, so that we immediately wiped them on our handkerchiefs. Suddenly there came the roar of engines. I stood paralysed. My DC-4 for Mexico City was flying directly overhead, then it curved round and out to sea, where it seemed to dissolve in the hot sky as though in a blue acid.

I said nothing.

I don't know how that day passed.

It passed.

Our train (Campeche–Palenque–Coatzocoalcos) was better than expected – a diesel engine with four air-conditioned carriages, so that we forgot the heat and along with the heat the stupidity of this whole journey.

'I wonder whether Joachim will recognize me?'

Every now and then our train would stop during the night on the open track, no one knew why, there was no light anywhere, from time to time a distant flash of lightning revealed that we were passing through a jungle, or sometimes a swamp, the lightning flashed behind a tangle of black trees, our locomotive hooted and hooted into the night, we couldn't open the window to see what was going on. . . . Suddenly it started off again – at twenty m.p.h., although the ground was as flat as a pancake and the line dead straight. Still, we were glad it was moving at all.

At one point I asked: 'Why did they get divorced?'

'Don't know,' he said. 'She became a Communist, I think.'

'Was that the reason?'

He yawned.

'I don't know,' he said. 'It wasn't a success. I never inquired.'

Once, when our train stopped again, I went to the carriage door and looked out. Outside was the heat we had forgotten, humid darkness and silence. I stepped down on to the footboard, the stillness was broken by flashes of lightning, a buffalo stood on the track in front of us, that was all. It stood as though stuffed, because it was dazzled by our headlamps, obstinately immovable. The sweat at once ran over my forehead and down my neck again. The locomotive hooted and hooted. All around us was undergrowth. After a few minutes the buffalo (or whatever it was) moved slowly out of the light of the headlamps, then I heard a rustling in the undergrowth, the snapping of branches, then a plop and it splashed around in the water out of sight.

After this we drove on.

'Have they any children?' I asked.

'One daughter.'

We settled down to sleep, our jackets under our heads, our legs stretched out on the empty seat opposite.

'Did you know her?'

'Yes,' I said. 'Why?'

Soon afterwards he fell asleep.

When morning broke, we were still in the brushwood; the early-morning sun shone over the low jungle horizon and white flocks of herons rose with a flapping of wings in front of our slow-moving train; there was brushwood without end, as far as the eye could see, with every now and then a group of Indian huts hidden among trees with aerial roots, an occasional isolated palm, but for the most part deciduous trees, acacias and others I didn't know, above all bushes and antediluvian ferns; the place was teeming with sulphur-yellow birds and the sun shone once more as though behind smoked glass, you could see the heat-haze.

I had been dreaming (not of Hanna!).

The next time we stopped on the open track it was Palenque, a little halt at which no one got out or in except us, a small shed beside the line, a signal, that was all, not even a double track (if I remember rightly); we asked three people where Palenque was.

The sweat immediately began to pour again.

The train drove on, leaving us standing there with our luggage as though at the end of the world, or at least at the end of civilization, and of the jeep that was supposed to take the gentleman from Düsseldorf straight to the plantation there was, of course, not a sign.

'Here we are.'

I laughed.

All the same, there was a narrow road, and, after a pretty exhausting half hour, children emerged from the bushes and later a donkey-driver, who took our luggage, an Indian of course. All I kept was my yellow briefcase with the zip-fastener.

For five days we were suspended in Palenque.

We were suspended in hammocks, with beer within reach all the time, sweating as though sweating was our purpose in life, incapable of coming to any decision, quite contented actually, because the beer here was excellent, YUCATECA, better than the beer in the uplands. We lay suspended in our hammocks and drank, so that we could sweat better, and I couldn't think what we really wanted.

We wanted a jeep.

If we didn't keep telling ourselves this all the time, we forgot about it, and apart from this we said very little all day long, a curious state.

A jeep, yes, but where from?

Talking only made us thirsty.

The landlord of our tiny hotel (the Lacroix) had a Land Rover, obviously the only vehicle in Palenque, but he needed it himself to fetch beer and guests from the railway station, people interested in Indian ruins, pyramid-lovers; at the moment there was only one of them there, a young American who talked too much, but fortunately he was out all day – looking at the ruins, which he thought we ought to look at too.

Not on your life!

Every step set the sweat pouring, which immediately had to be replaced with beer, and the only way to exist was to lie motionless in the hammock with bare feet, smoking; apathy was the only possible state; even a rumour that the plantation across the frontier had been abandoned months ago did not stir us; Herbert and I looked at one another and drank our beer.

Our only chance was the Land Rover.

It stood outside the hotel day after day.

But, as I have said, the hotel-keeper needed it.

Only after sunset (the sun didn't really set, it simply wilted away in the haze) did it become cooler, so that we could at least joke. About the future of the German cigar. I found the whole thing ludicrous, our trip and everything. Native uprising! I didn't believe that for a moment; the Indians were far too gentle, too peaceable, positively childlike. They squatted for whole evenings in their white straw hats on the earth, motionless as toadstools, content without light, silent. The sun and moon were enough light for them, an effeminate race, eerie but innocuous.

Herbert asked what I thought had happened.

Nothing.

What should we do? he asked.

Take a shower.

I showered from morning to evening, I hate sweat, because it makes me feel like a sick man. (I've never been ill in my life, except for measles.) I think Herbert was rather hurt that I had no suggestions to make, but it was much too hot. He himself made the craziest suggestions.

'Let's go to the cinema,' he said.

As if there was a cinema in this little cluster of Indian huts! He got quite angry when I laughed at him.

There was not a drop of rain.

Lightning flashed every evening, it was our only entertainment in the evenings, Palenque had a diesel motor that generates electricity, but it was turned off at 9 p.m., so there we were in the darkness of the jungle and all we could see was the lightning, bluish like a quartz lamp, and the red glow-worms, and later a slimy-looking moon, there were no stars to be seen, it was too hazy for that. ... Joachim simply didn't write any letters, because it was too hot, I could well understand that; he lay suspended in his hammock like us, yawning, or he was dead. ... There was nothing to do, anyhow, but wait till we could get a jeep and cross the frontier and see for ourselves.

Herbert yelled at me:

'A jeep! Where from?'

A few minutes afterwards he was snoring.

Apart from this, silence reigned most of the time, once the diesel generator had been turned off; a horse grazed in the moonlight and in the same enclosure a deer, but the deer made no sound, there was also a black sow and a turkey that couldn't bear the lightning and squawked, and also some geese that started cackling when the turkey set them off, there would be a sudden alarm, then silence again with lightning flashing across the flat landscape, only the grazing horse we heard all night long.

I thought about Joachim.

But what was I thinking?

I was simply awake.

Only our ruin-lover chattered a lot; it was quite interesting when you listened to him – about Toltecs, Zapotecs and Aztecs, who built temples yet hadn't discovered the wheel. He came from Boston and was a musician. At times he got on my nerves, like all artists who think themselves loftier or more profound beings simply because they didn't know what electricity is.

In the end I, too, fell asleep.

Every morning I was woken by a curious noise, half mechanical, half musical, a sound which I couldn't explain, not loud, but as frenzied as crickets, metallic, monotonous; it must be mechanical in origin, but I couldn't guess what it was, and later, when we went to breakfast in the village, it was silent, nothing to be seen. We were the only guests in the only inn, where we always ordered the same thing – *huevos a la mexicana*, terribly peppery, but presumably wholesome, together with tortilla and beer. The Indian proprietress, a matron with black pigtails, took us for archaeologists. Her hair resembled plumage; it was black with a bluish-green sheen. She had ivory teeth, that showed when she smiled, and soft black eyes.

'Ask her,' said Herbert, 'whether she knows my brother and when she last saw him!'

There wasn't much to be got out of her.

'She remembers a car,' I said. 'That's all.'

The parrot didn't know anything either.

GRACIAS, HEE-HEE!

I spoke Spanish to him.

HEE-HEE, GRACIAS, HEE-HEE!

On the third or fourth morning, while we were having breakfast in the usual way, gaped at by a crowd of Maya children who didn't beg but merely stood by our table and every now and then laughed, Herbert developed the fixed idea that somewhere in this miserable hamlet, if we only looked hard enough, there must be a jeep – behind some hut, somewhere in the thickets of gourds, bananas and maize. I left him to it. It struck me as crazy, like everything else, but I didn't care, I lay suspended in my hammock and Herbert didn't show up all day long.

I was even too lazy to take films.

Apart from beer, YUCATECA, which was excellent but flat, there was only rum in Palenque, rotten stuff, and Coca-Cola which I can't stand.

I drank and slept.

Anyhow, I spent hours thinking of nothing.

Herbert, who didn't return till dusk, pale with exhaustion, had discovered a brook and bathed; he had also discovered two men with curved sabres (so he asserted) walking through the maize, Indians with white trousers and white straw hats, just like the villagers – but carrying curved sabres.

Not a word about the jeep, of course!

I believe he was scared.

I shaved while there was still electric current, and Herbert told me all about his time in the Caucasus again, his horror stories about Ivan, which I knew already; later, as there was no more beer, we went to the cinema, accompanied by our ruin-lover, who knew his Palenque – there really was a cinema, a shed with a corrugated iron roof. The first film was Harold Lloyd climbing up and down walls in the manner of the twenties, the main film, love and passion among the Mexican smart set, adultery with a Cadillac and a Browning and plenty of evening dresses and marble. We doubled up with laughter, while the four or five Indians squatted motionless in front of the crumpled screen, their great straw hats on their heads, perhaps satisfied, perhaps not, you can never tell, they are so impassive, Mongolian. ... Our new friend, a Boston musician, as I mentioned, an American of French origin, was thrilled with Yucatan and couldn't understand why we were not interested in ruins; he asked what we were doing here.

We just shrugged our shoulders and looked at one another, each one leaving it to the other to say that we were waiting for a jeep.

I don't know what he must have thought of us.

Rum has the advantage that you don't break into a sweat as after every glass of beer; on the other hand you wake up with a headache next morning, when the incomprehensible noise starts off again, half piano, half machine-gun, and accompanied by singing – it went on every day between 6 and 7 a.m., and every day I decided to look into it, but I always forgot about it as the day wore on.

You forget everything here.

On one occasion – we wanted to bathe, but Herbert couldn't find his legendary brook and we suddenly found ourselves among the ruins – we came across our musician at work. Among the stones, which were supposed to represent a temple, the heat was unbearable. The only thing he was worried about was keeping the drops of sweat off his paper! He scarcely greeted us; we were disturbing him. His work consisted in placing tracing paper over the stone reliefs and then rubbing a black crayon this way and that for hours on end, a crazy way of obtaining a copy of anything; but he insisted that you couldn't photograph these hieroglyphs and grinning deities, they would be dead at once. We left him.

I'm no art historian.

After climbing around the pyramids for a while out of sheer boredom (the steps are far too steep, the relation between height and width is exactly the reverse of what it should be, so that you get out of breath), I lay down, dizzy from the heat, in the shadow of some so-called palace, with my arms and legs stretched out, breathing.

The humid air . . .

The slimy sun . . .

I had made up my mind to go back on my own if we didn't get hold of a jeep tomorrow. It was more sultry than ever, damp and musty; birds with long blue tails were flitting in all directions; someone had used the temple as a lavatory, hence the flies. I tried to sleep. The flitting wings and animal cries made the place sound like a zoo; you couldn't tell what creatures were whistling and screeching and warbling, it was a din like modern music, they might have been monkeys, or birds, or maybe some feline species, it was impossible to tell, they might have been in rut or terrified, you couldn't tell that either.

I could feel my stomach. (I was smoking too much.)

At one time, in the eleventh or thirteenth century, a whole city is supposed to have stood here, said Herbert, a Maya city.

So what?

To my question whether he still believed in the future of the German cigar, Herbert returned no answer; he was snoring, having finished talking about the religion of the Mayas, art and stuff like that ...

I let him snore.

I took my shoes off, snakes or no snakes, I needed air, I had palpitations from the heat, I was astounded by our tracing-paper artist, who could work in the blazing sun and gave up his holidays and his savings to bring home hieroglyphs which no one could decipher.

People are funny.

A race like these Mayas, who hadn't discovered the wheel and built pyramids and temples in the jungle, where everything becomes smothered in moss and crumbles with damp – what for?

I couldn't understand myself.

I should have landed in Caracas a week ago and today (at the latest) I ought to have been back in New York. Instead of that I was stuck here – for the sake of saying hello to a friend of my youth, who had married the girl friend of my youth.

What for?

We were waiting for the Land Rover that brought our ruin-artist here every day and took him back again around evening with his rolls of tracing paper. I decided to wake Herbert and tell him I was going off with the next train to leave Palenque.

The flitting birds ...

Never an aeroplane!

Every time I turned my head to one side to avoid seeing the smoked-glass sky, it was as if I was in the sea, our pyramid an island or a ship, with the sea on all sides; and yet it was nothing but undergrowth, unending, greenish-grey, flat as an ocean – undergrowth.

Above it the full moon, lilac in the daylight.

Herbert was still snoring away.

It's amazing how they got these blocks of stone here, when they weren't acquainted with the wheel and therefore had no pulleys. They didn't know the arch either. Apart from the decorations, which didn't appeal to me anyhow, because I like functionalism, I found these ruins extremely primitive – unlike our ruin-lover, who liked the Mayas precisely because they had no technology, but gods instead. He thought it delightful that they began a new era every two hundred and fifty years, smashed up all their pots and pans, put out all their fires, then relit them all over the country from the fire in the temple and made fresh pots and pans. A people that simply abandoned their cities (intact) and moved on, for religious reasons, and after fifty or a hundred miles built a completely new temple-city somewhere in this unchanging jungle – he thought it pregnant with significance, though uneconomic, a sign of great depth of spirit, that was his serious opinion.

Sometimes it made me think of Hanna.

When I woke Herbert, he sprang to his feet. What was the matter? When he saw that nothing was the matter, he started snoring again – to avoid being bored.

Not a sound of an engine!

I tried to picture what it would be like if there were suddenly no more engines as in the days of the Mayas. One has to think about something. I felt a rather childish amazement at the way in which they had shifted these blocks of stone: they simply built ramps and then dragged the blocks up them with an idiotic expenditure of manpower, that was what made it so primitive. On the other hand their astronomy. According to the ruin-lover, their calendar reckoned the solar year at 365.2420 days, instead of 365.2422 days; nevertheless, for all their mathematical knowledge, they never evolved a technology and were therefore condemned to decline and disappear.

Our Land Rover at last!

The miracle happened when our ruin-lover heard that we had to cross over into Guatemala. He was wildly enthusiastic. He took out his little calendar and counted the remaining days of his vacation. Guatemala, he said, was teeming with Maya settlements, some of them barely excavated, and if we could take him with us he would do everything in his power to get the Land Rover, which we couldn't get, on the strength of his friendship with the landlord of the Lacroix Hotel – and he did get it.

(At a hundred pesos a day.)

It was Sunday when we packed, a hot night with a slimy moon, and the queer noise that had woken me every morning turned out to be music, the clatter of an antiquated marimba, hammer taps without resonance, a ghastly kind of music, positively epileptic. It was some festival connected with the full moon. They had practised every morning before going to work in the fields, so that now they could play for dancing, five Indians who struck their instrument with whirling hammers, a kind of wooden xylophone, as long as a table. I overhauled the engine to avoid a breakdown in the jungle and had no time to watch the dancing; I was lying underneath our Land Rover. The girls were sitting in rows round the market place, most of them with a baby at their brown breasts; the dancers sweated and drank coconut milk. As the night passed, more and more seemed to arrive, whole tribes; the girls were not wearing their everyday clothes, but American frocks in honour of their moon, a fact that agitated Marcel, our artist, for several hours. I had other worries. We had no arms, no compass, nothing. I'm not interested in folklore. I packed our Land Rover, after all someone had to, and I was glad to do it in order to get out of here.

*

Hanna had to leave Germany and came to study art history

with Professor Wölfflin, a subject in which I took no interest, but apart from this we understood one another immediately, without thinking about marriage. Hanna didn't think about marriage either. We were too young, as I have already said, quite apart from my parents, who found Hanna a very pleasant person, but were worried about what would happen to my career if I married a girl who was half Jewish, a worry that angered, indeed infuriated, me. I was quite ready to marry Hanna, I felt under an obligation to do so because of the times we were living in. Her father, a professor at Munich, was taken into custody just then, those were the days of what people referred to at the time as 'atrocity stories', and of course I wouldn't leave Hanna in the lurch. I wasn't a coward, quite apart from the fact that we really loved each other. I remember those days clearly, there was a party rally at Nuremberg, we sat by the radio, the race laws were promulgated. It was really Hanna who didn't want to get married then; I was perfectly willing. When I heard from Hanna that she had to leave Switzerland in fourteen days I was an officer in the army at Thun; I at once travelled to Zurich and went with Hanna to the aliens office, where my uniform made no difference, but at least we saw the head of the department. I can still remember how he looked at the letter Hanna showed him and then sent for her dossier; Hanna was sitting, I was standing. Then his well-meaning question as to whether the young lady was my fiancée, and our embarrassment. We must understand that Switzerland was a small country, no room for countless refugees, right of asylum, but Hanna had had time enough to make arrangements for her emigration. Then finally the dossier arrived and it turned out that it didn't concern Hanna at all, but a refugee with the same name who had already emigrated overseas. Everyone felt relieved. In the anteroom I was picking up my officer's gloves and my officer's cap, when Hanna was called back to the counter. Hanna went white in the face. She had to pay ten centimes, postage for the letter wrongly sent to her address. She was wildly indignant. I thought it a joke. Unfortunately I had to go back the same evening to my recruits at Thun. During that journey I made up my mind to marry Hanna, if ever her residence permit were withdrawn. Soon afterwards (if I remember rightly) her old father died in prison. I had made up my mind, as I have said, but I never got round to it. I don't really know why. Hanna was always very sensitive and moody, an unpredictable temperament – manic-depressive, as Joachim said. Though Joachim had only seen her once or twice; Hanna didn't want to have anything to do with Germans. I swore to her that Joachim, my friend, was no Nazi; but it was no use. I understood her mistrust, but she didn't make things easy for me, apart from the fact that our interests weren't always the same. I called her a sentimentalist and arty crafty. She called me Homo Faber. Sometimes we had out-and-out rows, for example when we came out of the theatre, which Hanna was always making me go to; on the one hand Hanna had Communist leanings, which I couldn't bear, and on the other a tendency to mysticism, or to put it less kindly, hysteria. Now, I am a man who has both feet on the ground. Nevertheless, we were very happy together, it seems to me, and I really don't know why we didn't marry. We just didn't get around to it. Unlike my father, I wasn't anti-semitic, as far as I can remember; I was simply so young, like most men under thirty, too immature to become a father, I was still working on my dissertation, as I have said, and living with my parents, which Hanna couldn't understand at all. We always used to meet in her room. Then came the offer from Escher-Wyss, a chance in a million for a young engineer, and what worried me about it was not the climate in Baghdad, but Hanna in Zurich. She was expecting a child at that time. I heard her revelation on the very day on which I came from my first interview with

Escher-Wyss, having made up my mind to take the job in Baghdad as soon as possible. I still contest her assertion that I was scared to death. I merely asked: Are you sure? A perfectly matter-of-fact and reasonable question. It was only her certainty that made me feel duped. I asked: Have you been to a doctor? Also a reasonable and permissible question. She knew for sure! I said: Let's wait another fortnight. She laughed because she was perfectly certain, and I couldn't help assuming that she had known for a long time and hadn't told me; that was the only reason I felt duped. I put my hand on her hand, at the moment I couldn't think of anything much to say, that's true; I drank coffee and smoked. Her disappointment! I didn't dance with joy at the prospect of becoming a father, it's true, the political situation was far too serious for that. I asked: Do you know a doctor you can go to? Of course I only meant, to have an examination. Hanna nodded. That's no problem, she said, that can be arranged. I asked: What do you mean? Later, Hanna asserted that I was relieved she wasn't going to have the child, positively delighted, and that's why I put my arm round her shoulder when she cried. She was the one who didn't want to talk about it any more, and then I told her about Escher-Wyss, about the job in Baghdad, about an engineer's professional prospects in general. This wasn't aimed at her child at all. I even told her how much I should be earning in Baghdad. My very words were: If you want to have your child, then of course we must get married. Later she reproached me for having said 'must'. I asked her frankly: Do you want to get married or don't you? She shook her head, and I didn't know where I stood. I discussed the matter at length with Joachim, while we were playing chess; Joachim told me about the medical side of it, which of course was no problem, then about the legal side, which was no problem either if you knew how to get hold of the necessary certificate; then he filled his pipe and stared at the chessboard, for Joachim was fundamentally opposed to giving advice. He promised his help (he was a medical student in the middle of his finals) in case we, the girl and I, should need his help. I was very grateful, rather embarrassed, but glad he didn't make a great fuss about it. He merely said: It's your move. I told Hanna the whole thing was no problem. It was Hanna who suddenly broke it all off; she packed her bag, suddenly seized with the crazy idea of going back to Munich. I planted myself in front of her and tried to make her see sense. All she said was: It's all over. I had said 'your child', instead of 'our child'. That was what Hanna could not forgive me.

*

The distance from Palenque to the plantation was barely seventy miles as the crow flies, which meant about a hundred miles by car – a negligible journey if there had been anything approaching a road, which of course there wasn't; the only road going in that direction stopped at the ruins, simply disappearing into moss and ferns.

Nevertheless, we made progress.

Thirty-seven miles the first day.

We took turns driving.

Nineteen miles the second day.

We simply kept heading south-east, but of course moving in a zig-zag, cutting through any gaps in the undergrowth, which is actually not so dense and impenetrable as it looks from a distance; there were clearings everywhere, and even herds, but without herdsmen, and fortunately no large swamps.

Flashes of lightning.

Rain never fell.

What set my nerves on edge was the rattle of our petrol tins; I stopped several times and tightened the ropes, but after half an hour of driving over roots and rotting tree trunks they were rattling again.

Marcel kept whistling.

Although he was sitting at the back, where he was bounced from side to side all the time, he whistled like a kid on a school spree. When he wasn't whistling, he sang a French children's song for hours on end.

Il Etait Un Petit Navire ...

Herbert kept rather quiet.

We spoke very little about Joachim.

What Herbert couldn't stand were the zopilotes; yet they do us no harm at all as long as we are alive, they merely stink, as is only to be expected of vultures, they are ugly and you always come across them in flocks, it's almost impossible to frighten them away once they get to work, it's no use blowing your horn, they just flap their wings and hop round the carcass they have ripped open, refusing to give it up. . . . On one occasion, when Herbert was at the wheel, he was seized by an absolute fury; he suddenly put his foot down and drove straight into the black pack, into the middle and right through, so that black feathers rained down on all sides.

Afterwards it was all over the wheels.

The sweetish stench kept us company for hours, until we dealt with it. The stuff stuck in the treads of the tyres and there was nothing for it but to scrape it laboriously out by hand, groove by groove. Fortunately we had rum! Without rum I think we should have turned back – on the third day – not out of fear, but out of common sense.

We had no idea where we were.

Somewhere on the eighteenth parallel.

Marcel either sang *Il Etait Un Petit Navire* or chattered all night long – about Cortez and Montezuma (I didn't mind that, after all, it's historical) or about the decline of the white race (it was too hot and too humid to argue), about the disastrous pseudo-victory of the western technologist (he called Cortez a technologist, because he possessed gunpowder!), about the Indian soul and a lot of other rubbish, a whole

54

lecture about the return of the old gods (after the H-bomb had been dropped!) and about death becoming extinct (his very words!) thanks to penicillin, about the retreat of the soul from all the civilized regions of the earth, the soul in the *maquis* and so on. Herbert woke up at the word *maquis*, which he understood, and asked: 'What's he talking about?' – 'Highbrow tripe,' I said, and we let him go on about his theory of America, which he said had no future, '*The American Way of Life* was an attempt to cosmeticize life, but you couldn't cosmeticize life . . .'

I tried to sleep.

I only lost my temper when Marcel started to talk about my work, that is to say about UNESCO, saying the technologist was the final guise of the white missionary, industrialization the last gospel of a dying race and living standards a substitute for a purpose in living . . .

I asked him if he was a Communist.

Marcel denied it.

On the third day, when we were once more driving through the bush with no track to follow, simply heading in the direction of Guatemala, I had had enough.

I was for turning back.

'Because it's idiotic,' I said, 'just to drive on at random until we've no petrol left.'

Herbert took out his map.

What got on my nerves were the newts in every pool, a seething mass of newts in every one-day puddle – all this procreation, this stench of fertility, of blossoming decay.

Wherever you spat it germinated!

I knew this 1: 500,000 map that didn't show a thing, even under the magnifying glass, nothing but white paper – a blue river, a dead-straight frontier, a line of latitude in the empty white . . . I was for turning back. I wasn't afraid (what of?), but there was no point. We went on simply to please Herbert; unfortunately, for soon afterwards we did indeed come to a river, or rather a river bed, which could only be the Usumancinta, the border between Mexico and Guatemala, dry in some places and in others full of water that didn't seem to be flowing; we couldn't cross at this point, but there must be places where you could get across without a bridge, and Herbert wouldn't wait, although I wanted to bathe, he drove along the bank until we came to a point where we could cross, and Joachim (as we learned later) had also crossed.

I had a bathe.

Marcel bathed too, and we floated on our backs in the water with our mouths shut to avoid swallowing any; the water was warm and murky and stank, every movement left bubbles behind, but still it was water; the irritating things were the innumerable dragonflies and Herbert, who kept wanting to move on, and the thought that there might be snakes.

Herbert stayed on land.

Our Land Rover stood up to its axles in the slippery marl (or whatever it was), Herbert was filling the petrol tank.

There were swarms of butterflies.

When I saw a rusty petrol tin in the water, which suggested that Joachim (who else?) had also once filled his tank here, I said nothing, but went on bathing, while Herbert tried to get our Land Rover out of the slippery marl . . .

I was for turning back.

I stayed in the water, although it suddenly disgusted me, the insects, the bubbles on the brown water, the lazy flicker of the sunlight, a sky full of vegetation when you lay on your back and looked up, fronds with yard-long leaves, motionless, in between them the filigree of acacia, lichen, aerial roots, motionless, every now and then a red bird that flew across the river; apart from this, deathly silence (when Herbert wasn't revving up) beneath a whitish sky, the sun as though bedded in cotton wool, clammy and hot, hazy with a circular rainbow.

I was for turning back.

'Because it's crazy,' I said, 'because we'll never find this plantation.'

I was for taking a vote.

Marcel was also in favour of turning back, because his vacation was drawing to an end; when Herbert had finally succeeded in getting the Land Rover across to the other bank, it was only a question of convincing him of the stupidity of going on when there was absolutely no trail to follow. At first he cursed me, because he couldn't contradict my arguments, then he fell silent and listened and I had just about won him round – when Marcel suddenly put a spoke in the wheel.

'Voilà,' he shouted, 'les traces d'une Nash.'

We thought he was joking.

'Mais regardez,' he cried, 'sans blague ...'

In places the crusty tracks had been partially washed away, so that they might have been cart tracks; at other places, according to the nature of the soil, we could clearly recognize the tyre pattern.

Now we had our trail.

Otherwise I shouldn't have gone on and everything would have turned out differently – this is a thought I cannot get out of my mind.

Now there was no turning back.

(Unfortunately!)

On the morning of the fourth day we saw two Indians crossing a field with curved sabres in their hands, just like the two Herbert had seen in Palenque and taken for murderers; their curved sabres were nothing but sickles.

Then came the first tobacco fields.

The hope of arriving before nightfall made us more on edge than ever, on top of this heat, tobacco on all sides with ditches in between, human handiwork, dead straight, but no human being anywhere.

We had lost the trail again.

Again we searched for the tread pattern.

Soon the sun went down; we stood on our Land Rover and whistled with our fingers in our mouths, as loudly as we could. We couldn't be far away. We whistled and hooted, while the sun was already sinking into the green tobacco – as though bloated, looking in the haze like a blister filled with blood, repulsive, like a kidney or something of that sort.

The moon was just the same.

It would have been the last straw if we had now lost one another in the dusk, as each of us trudged off in a different direction looking for tyre marks. We divided the ground up into areas and examined one each. Whichever of us found something looking like a tyre track was to whistle.

Only the birds whistled.

We went on searching by moonlight, until Herbert stumbled on the zopilotes, zopilotes on a dead donkey – he let out a yell and fled and threw stones at the black birds, uncontrollable in his rage. It was horrible. The donkey's eyes had been pecked out, leaving two red holes, so had the tongue; now they were trying, as Herbert threw his stones, to drag the entrails out through the anus.

This was our fourth night.

We had nothing left to drink.

I was exhausted, the earth felt as though it were heated, I sat there with my head in my hands, sweating in the bluish moonlight. There were glow-worms everywhere.

Herbert paced up and down.

Only Marcel slept.

At one point I suddenly heard no more footsteps and looked over to Herbert – he was standing by the dead donkey, he wasn't throwing stones at the rustling birds, just standing watching.

They gorged themselves all night long.

When the moon sank at last into the tobacco, so that the

damp mist over the field ceased to look like milk, I finally slept; but not for long.

There was the sun again !

The donkey lay gaping open, the zopilotes had eaten their fill and were perched on the trees round about, as though stuffed, when we set off again with no path to follow; Herbert, as the representative and nephew of Hencke-Bosch & Co. Ltd, to whom these fields belonged, assumed responsibility and the steering wheel, still without a word, and drove straight through the tobacco; it was absurd, we left a trail of broken tobacco plants behind us, but we had no alternative, since our repeated hooting and whistling brought no answer.

The sun was rising.

Then a group of Indians, employees of Hencke-Bosch & Co. Ltd, Düsseldorf, came and told us their señor was dead. I had to translate, beause Herbert knew no Spanish. What did they mean, dead? They shrugged their shoulders. Their señor was dead, they said, and one of them showed us the way by running alongside our Land Rover at the Indian jogtrot.

The rest went on working.

So there was no question of an uprising.

It was an American Quonset hut, roofed with corrugated iron, and the only door was bolted from inside. We shouted and knocked for Joachim to let us in.

'Nuestro señor es muerto.'

I fetched the spanner from our Land Rover, and Herbert broke open the door. I wouldn't have recognized him. Fortunately he had done it behind closed windows, there were zopilotes on the trees all round, zopilotes on the roof, but they couldn't get in through the windows. You could see him through the windows. Nevertheless, the Indians went to work every day and never thought of breaking down the door and taking down the hanged man. He had done it with wire. I wondered where his radio, which we immediately switched off, was getting the electric current from, but that wasn't the important thing at the moment . . .

We photographed and buried him.

The Indians (as already stated in my report to the board of directors) carried out all Herbert's instructions, although at that time he spoke no Spanish, and at once recognized Herbert as their immediate superior . . . I sacrificed another day and a half to convincing Herbert that there could be no question of an uprising and that his brother had simply been unable to stand up to the climate, which I could well understand; I don't know what Herbert had got into his head, he refused to be persuaded; for his part, he was determined to stand up to the climate. We had to go back. We felt sorry for Herbert, but it was quite impossible for us to stay, apart from the fact that there was no point; Marcel had to get back to his work in Boston, and I had to move on, or rather back along the route Palenque–Campeche–Mexico, to continue my flight, quite apart from the fact that we had undertaken to return our Land Rover to the friendly landlord of the Lacroix in a week at the outside. I had to get to my turbines. I don't know how Herbert imagined he would manage, he couldn't even speak Spanish, as I have said, and I found it uncomradely, positively irresponsible, to leave him there with no other white man; we begged him to come back with us, but in vain. Herbert had the Nash 55, which I looked over; the car was standing in an Indian hut, protected from the rain only by a roof of leaves; it obviously hadn't been used for a long time and was scratched and filthy, but it went. I overhauled it myself. At that time the engine was in working order, although clogged up; I tested it out and there was plenty of petrol. Otherwise, naturally, we shouldn't have left Herbert alone. We simply had no time, neither Marcel nor I; Marcel had to get back to his symphony players, we both had our jobs, whether Herbert could grasp that or not – he shrugged his shoulders without contradicting, and scarcely waved when Marcel and I were sitting in the Land Rover giving him a last chance to come with us; he shook his head. On top of everything it looked as though a storm was blowing up, and we had to get going while our trail was still there to follow back.

*

It still puzzles me why Hanna and Joachim married and why she never let me, the father of her child, know that this child had come into the world.

I can only report what I know.

It was the time when the Jewish passports were withdrawn. I had sworn not to leave Hanna in the lurch and I stuck to my promise. Joachim was willing to act as witness to the marriage. My worried middle-class parents were also glad we didn't want a wedding with coaches and a lot of to-do; only Hanna was still doubtful whether it was right for us to marry, right for me. I took our papers to the appropriate office, our wedding announcement was in the papers. Even if we get divorced, I told myself, Hanna will remain Swiss and in possession of a passport. Time was short, because I had to start my job in Baghdad. It was a Saturday morning when we eventually – after a queer breakfast with my parents, who, when it came to the point, missed the sound of wedding bells – went into the town hall to go through the marriage ceremony. The place was teeming with couples waiting to get married, as always on a Saturday, that was why we had to wait so long, we sat in the antechamber, all in our everyday clothes, surrounded by white brides and bridegrooms who looked liked waiters. I thought nothing of it when Hanna went outside; we talked, we smoked. When the registry official finally called us, Hanna wasn't there. We looked for her and found her outside on the banks of the Limmat; we couldn't shift her, she refused to go into the registry office.

She couldn't! I talked to her encouragingly while the clocks all around struck eleven; I begged Hanna to look at the situation quite objectively; but in vain. She shook her head and wept. I was only marrying her to prove I wasn't an anti-semite, she said, and there was just nothing to be done. The following week, my last in Zurich, was horrible. It was Hanna who didn't want to get married, and I had no choice, I had to go to Baghdad under the terms of my contract. Hanna went with me to the station, and we said good-bye. Hanna promised that as soon as I had left she would go to Joachim, who had promised his medical aid, and it was on this understanding that we parted; it was agreed that our child should not be born.

I never heard from her again.

That was in 1936.

I asked Hanna at the time what she thought of my friend Joachim. She thought him a nice chap. It never entered my head that Hanna and Joachim might marry.

*

My stay in Venezuela (two months ago today) lasted only two days, for the turbines were still at the docks, all packed up in crates, and there could be no question of assembly.

April 20th – Flew from Caracas.

April 21st – Landed at Idlewild, New York.

Ivy hooked me the moment I stepped off the plane, she had found out when I was arriving and there was no escaping her. Hadn't she received my letter? She kissed me without replying and already knew that I had to fly to Paris in a week on official business; she smelled of whisky.

I didn't utter a word.

We got into our Studebaker, and Ivy drove to my flat. Not a word about my desert letter! Ivy had brought flowers, although I don't care for flowers, and a lobster, and sauterne –

to celebrate my escape from the desert – and more kisses as I went through my mail.

I hate farewells.

I hadn't reckoned with seeing Ivy again, and certainly not in this flat, which she called 'our' flat.

Maybe I was a long time in the shower . . .

The row began when Ivy came in with a bath towel; I threw her out – violently, unfortunately, for she loved violence, it gave her an excuse to bite me . . .

As luck would have it, the phone rang.

After I had made a date with Dick, who congratulated me on my forced landing, a date to play chess, Ivy called me a brute, an egotist, a monster with absolutely no feelings . . .

Of course, I laughed.

She struck me with both fists, sobbing, but I took care not to use force, because that was what she wanted.

Maybe Ivy loved me.

(I've never been certain with women.)

A quarter of an hour later, when I rang Dick and told him that unfortunately I couldn't come after all, he had already set out the pieces; I had to apologize, which was embarrassing. I couldn't tell him why I wasn't able to come, I merely said I would much rather play chess.

Ivy started sobbing again.

That was at 6 p.m., and I knew exactly how this long evening would pass if we didn't go out; I suggested a French restaurant, then a Chinese one, then a Swedish one. All in vain. Ivy coolly told me she wasn't hungry. But I was, I told her. She pointed out the lobster in the refrigerator and also her casual frock, which wasn't suitable for a smart restaurant. What did I think of her frock, by the way? I had already picked up our lobster with the intention of throwing it into the incinerator – I wasn't going to be bullied by a lobster . . .

Ivy immediately promised to be sensible.

I put the lobster back into the refrigerator, Ivy agreed to the Chinese restaurant; only, as I had to admit, she certainly had to make up her face after all those tears.

I waited.

My flat, on Central Park West, had been costing me too much for a long time. Two rooms and a roof garden, a unique location, no doubt of that, but much too expensive if one wasn't in love.

Ivy asked when I was flying to Paris.

I didn't answer.

I was standing outside sorting my last films in readiness to have them developed, writing labels on the spools, as usual. ... I didn't feel like talking about Joachim's death, Ivy didn't know him, Joachim had been my one real friend.

Why was I so taciturn?

Dick, for example, was a nice fellow, also a chess player, highly educated, I believe, anyhow more educated than I am, a witty chap whom I admired (only at chess was I his equal), or at least envied, one of those people who could save your life without becoming your intimate friend on that account.

Ivy was still combing her hair.

I told her about my forced landing.

Ivy was doing her eyelashes.

The mere fact that we were going out together again, after parting in writing, made me furious. But Ivy seemed to have no idea that we had parted!

I suddenly felt I'd had enough.

Ivy was varnishing her finger nails and humming.

All of a sudden I heard myself on the telephone, inquiring about a passage to Europe by boat, it didn't matter what line, the quicker the better.

'What do you mean, by boat?' asked Ivy.

It was very unlikely that I should be able to get a passage to Europe at this time of the year, and I don't know what suddenly made me decide not to fly (perhaps only the fact that Ivy was humming and acting as though nothing had happened). I was surprised myself. I was lucky, a cabin-class booking had just been cancelled – Ivy heard me take it and jumped up to interrupt me; but I had already put down the receiver.

'It's okay,' I said.

Ivy was speechless, which I enjoyed; I lit myself a cigarette.

Ivy had caught the time of my departure.

'Eleven o'clock tomorrow morning.'

I repeated it.

'Are you ready?' I asked, holding her coat in the usual way, ready to go out with her. Ivy stared at me, then she suddenly threw her coat across the room and stamped her foot, beside herself with rage. . . . Ivy had arranged to spend a week in Manhattan, she now revealed, and my sudden decision not to fly, but to leave tomorrow by boat so as to reach Paris in a week's time as planned, upset her calculations.

I picked up her coat.

I had written and told her it was all over, she had it in black and white; she simply hadn't believed me. She thought she could lead me by the nose and that if we spent a week together everything would be as before, that's what she thought – and that was why I laughed.

Maybe I was mean.

So was she.

Her suspicion that I was afraid to fly was touching, and although, of course, I have never felt in the least afraid of flying I acted as though this was the explanation. I wanted to make things easier for her. I didn't want to be mean. I lied and told her (for the second time) all about my forced landing at Tamaulipas and, to make my decision understandable, how close we had come to . . .

'Oh honey,' she said, 'stop it!'

A fault in the fuel feed, which should never happen, of course, one single breakdown would be enough, I said, and what use would it be to me that out of 1,000 flights I had made, 999 would pass without incident; of what interest would it be to me that on the same day as I crashed in the sea, 999 planes made perfect landings?

She grew thoughtful.

So why not travel by sea for a change?

I worked out the odds until Ivy believed me, she actually sat down and admitted that she had never worked out the odds like that before; she could well understand my decision not to fly.

She begged my pardon.

I have flown more than 100,000 miles in my life, I should think, with no sign of a breakdown. There was no question of my being afraid of flying. I just pretended, until Ivy asked me never to fly again.

I had to swear . . .

Never again!

Ivy was funny – she wanted to read my hand; she suddenly believed in my fear of flying and was afraid for my life. I felt sorry for her, because she seemed to be completely serious when she spoke about my short line of life (and yet I'm already fifty!) and wept; as she deciphered my left hand, I stroked her hair with my right – which was a mistake.

I could feel her hot skull.

Ivy is twenty-six.

I promised to go and see a doctor and felt her tears on my left hand, it all seemed to me terribly sentimental, but there was nothing I could do about it, Ivy was like that by temperament, she believed what she said and although I, for my part, don't believe in fortune telling, naturally, not for a moment, I had to comfort her as though I had already crashed and been smashed to pieces and charred beyond recognition, I laughed of course, but I stroked her hair as you stroke and comfort a young widow, and kissed her . . .

Everything happened exactly as I had intended it shouldn't.

An hour later we were sitting side by side, Ivy in the dressing gown I had given her for Christmas, eating lobster and drinking sauterne; I hated her.

I hated myself.

Ivy was humming. As though contemptuously.

I had written to tell her it was all over, and she had my letter (I could see it) in her pocket.

Now she was having her revenge.

I was hungry, but the lobster revolted me. Ivy thought it heavenly, and I was revolted by her demonstrations of affection, her hand on my knee, her hand on my arm, her arm on my shoulder, her shoulder against my chest, her kiss when I poured out the wine, it was intolerable – I told her straight out that I hated her.

Ivy didn't believe it.

I stood at the window and hated every moment I had spent in this Manhattan, and especially my flat. I felt like setting fire to it. When I came back from the window Ivy still wasn't dressed, but she had prepared two grapefruits and asked whether I wanted coffee.

I told her to get dressed.

As she walked past me to put the water on for coffee, she turned her nose up at me. As though I were an idiot. Did I want to go to the cinema? she asked from the kitchen alcove, as though she were ready to come at once – in stockings and a dressing gown.

Now she was playing cat and mouse.

I controlled myself and I didn't say a word, I collected her shoes, her underclothes, all her odds and ends (I can't bear the sight of these pink things at the best of times) and threw

67

them into the next room, so that Ivy could go through her interminable toilet all over again.

Yes, I wanted to go to the cinema.

The coffee did me good.

My resolve to give up my flat was now unshakeable, and I told her so.

Ivy didn't contradict.

I felt a desire to shave, not because it was necessary, but just because I felt like it. To avoid waiting for Ivy. But my shaver was broken; I went from socket to socket – it wouldn't buzz.

Ivy thought I looked perfectly all right.

But that wasn't the point.

Ivy had her hat and coat on.

Of course I looked perfectly all right, quite apart from the fact that I had another shaver in the bathroom, it was older, but it worked; but that wasn't the point, as I said; I sat down and took the shaver to pieces. Any appliance can break down; it only worries me until I have found out why.

'Walter,' she said, 'I'm waiting.'

As though she had never kept me waiting!

'Technology!' she said – not only uncomprehendingly, as I'm used to hearing women speak of it, but positively scornfully, which didn't prevent me from taking the little appliance completely to pieces; I wanted to know what was wrong.

*

It was once again pure coincidence that decided the future, no more, a nylon thread in the little appliance – anyhow it was pure chance that we had not yet left the flat when the Compagnie Générale Transatlantique rang, the same call, probably, that I had heard about an hour ago, but hadn't been able to answer, a crucial call it was. My passage to Europe could only be booked if I called at once, by 10 p.m. at the latest, with my passport. All I mean is that if I hadn't taken the little appliance apart the call wouldn't have reached me and this would have meant that my voyage would never have taken place, at least not on the ship on which Sabeth was travelling, and we should never have met, my daughter and I.

*

An hour later I was sitting in a bar, my boat ticket in my pocket, down by the Hudson, cheerful, now that I had seen our ship, a gigantic tub with lighted port holes everywhere, masts and cranes and the red funnels in the floodlight – I was enjoying life like a youngster, as I hadn't done for a long time. My first sea voyage! I drank a beer and ate a sandwich, a man among men; a hamburger with plenty of mustard, because I felt hungry as soon as I was alone; I pushed my hat on to the back of my head, licked the froth from my lips and glanced at the boxing match on television. I was surrounded by dock labourers, most of them Negroes, I lit a cigarette and asked myself what I really expected from life when I was a youngster.

Ivy was waiting in the flat.

Unfortunately I had to go back, I still had to pack, but there was no hurry. I ate a second hamburger.

I thought of Joachim.

I felt as though I were beginning a new life, perhaps merely because I had never made a sea voyage before; anyhow, I was looking forward to my sea voyage.

I sat there till midnight.

I hoped Ivy wasn't waiting any longer, that she had lost patience and left my flat, angry with me because (as I very well knew) I had behaved like a heel; but there was no other way of getting rid of Ivy – I paid and walked all the way, to increase the chances of not meeting Ivy by half an hour; I knew she was tough. That was about all I did know about

Ivy. She was a Catholic, a model, she could take a joke about anything except the Pope, perhaps she was Lesbian, perhaps frigid, she felt the urge to seduce me because she thought I was an egotist, a monster, she wasn't stupid, but a bit perverse, it seemed to me, a bit queer, and yet she was a good kid when she didn't get sexy.... When I entered my flat she was sitting in her hat and coat, smiling; although I had kept her waiting over two hours, there were no reproaches.

'Everything okay?' she asked.

There was still some wine in the bottle.

'Everything okay,' I said.

Her ashtray was brimming over, her face was tear-stained, I filled our glasses as fairly as possible and apologized for what had gone before. Let bygones be bygones! I'm unbearable when I am overworked, and one is generally overworked.

Our sauterne was lukewarm.

When we clinked glasses, Ivy (who was standing) wished me a happy voyage, a happy life all around. Without a kiss. We drank standing, as at diplomatic receptions. All in all, I thought, we had had good times together, Ivy thought so too, our week-ends out on Fire Island, and our evenings on the roof garden here too.

'Let bygones be bygones,' said Ivy also.

She looked charming, but good sense personified, she had a boy's figure, only her bosom was very female, her hips narrow, as was right in a model.

So we stood and said good-bye.

I kissed her.

She refused to kiss me.

While I held her, wanting nothing but a last kiss, and felt her body, she turned her face away; I kissed her out of defiance, while Ivy smoked and refused to put her cigarette down, I kissed her ear, her taut throat, her temple, her bitter hair.

She stood like a tailor's dummy.

She not only smoked her cigarette as though it was her last, right down to the filter – in her other hand she held her empty glass.

I don't know how it happened again.

I believe Ivy wanted me to hate myself and seduced me merely to make me hate myself, and that was her joy, to humiliate me, the only joy I could give her.

There were times when she frightened me.

We sat there just as a few hours earlier.

Ivy wanted to sleep.

When I phoned Dick again – I couldn't think of any other solution – it was a long time past midnight, Dick was having a party of his own, I told him to come over with the whole gang. You could hear his party over the telephone, a confused uproar of drunken voices. I besought him. But Dick was adamant. Only when Ivy attached herself to the receiver did Dick consent to save me from being alone with Ivy.

I was dog tired.

Ivy combed her hair for the third time.

At last, when I had fallen asleep in the rocking chair, they arrived. Seven or nine men, of whom three were cripples who had to be carried in from the lift. One went on strike when he heard there was a woman present; that was too much for him or too little. Drunk as he was, he walked down the stairs, cursing, sixteen storeys.

Dick did the introductions:

'This is a friend of mine . . .'

I don't believe he knew the fellow himself, somebody was found to be missing. I explained that one of them had turned back; Dick felt responsible for seeing that none of his friends got lost and counted them on his fingers; after a lot of fuss, it turned out that one of them was still missing.

'He's lost,' said Dick, 'anyhow . . .'

Of course I tried to look at everything from the funny side, even when the Indian vase smashed to smithereens – and it wasn't even mine.

Ivy told me I had no sense of humour.

An hour later I still had no idea who these people were. One of them was supposed to be a famous acrobat. To prove it, he threatened to do a handstand on the balustrade of our sixteenth-floor balcony, which we were able to prevent; in the struggle a whisky bottle fell down over the front of the building – of course he wasn't an acrobat, they just said so to fool me, I don't know why. Fortunately the bottle didn't hit anyone. I went down at once, prepared to find a crowd of people, ambulance, blood, police who would arrest me. But there was nothing of the kind. When I came back into my flat they burst out laughing, saying no whisky bottle had fallen down at all.

I don't know what the truth was.

When I happened to go to the toilet the door was bolted. I fetched a screwdriver and prised it open. There was a fellow sitting on the floor smoking, who wanted to know what my name was.

It went on like this all night.

'In your company a man could die,' I said, 'a man could die and you wouldn't even notice, there's no trace of friendship, a man could die in your company!' I shouted. 'What the hell are we talking to each other for at all?' I shouted. 'What the hell's the point of this party,' I could hear myself shouting, 'if a man could die without your noticing?'

I was drunk.

It went on like this until morning – I don't know when they left the flat or how; only Dick still lay there.

By 9.30 a.m. I had to be on board.

I had a headache, I packed and was glad Ivy helped me, I was late, I asked her to make some good coffee, she behaved wonderfully and even came aboard with me. Of course she cried. I didn't know who Ivy had besides myself, apart from her husband; she had never mentioned her mother and father, I could only recall her curious remark, 'I'm just a dead-end kid.' She came from the Bronx, beyond this I really knew nothing about Ivy, to begin with I took her for a dancer, then for a tart, neither was right – I believe Ivy really did work as a model.

We were standing on deck.

Ivy in her humming-bird hat.

Ivy promised to see to everything in connection with the Studebaker. I gave her the keys. I thanked her as the siren blew and the loudspeaker kept telling visitors to leave the ship; I kissed her, because now Ivy really had to go, sirens were reverberating on all sides so that we had to stop our ears. Ivy was the last to cross the gangplank to land.

I waved.

I had to pull myself together, although I was glad when the heavy hawsers were cast off. It was a cloudless day. I was glad everything had gone off all right.

Ivy was also waving.

A good kid, I thought, although I have never understood Ivy; I was standing on the base of a crane as the black tug pulled us out stern first, the sirens blew again, I filmed (with my new telescopic lens) Ivy waving, until you could no longer distinguish faces with the naked eye. I filmed the whole process of leaving port, as long as we could see Manhattan, and then the gulls kept us company.

*

We shouldn't have buried Joachim in the earth (it often seems to me), we should have cremated him. But that couldn't be altered now. Marcel was absolutely right: fire is clean, earth is mire after a single storm (as we found out on our return journey), decay filled with seed, as slippery as vaseline, pools in the red of dawn like pools of filthy blood, menstrual blood, pools full of newts, nothing but black heads with jerking tails like a seething mass of spermatozoa, just like that – horrible.

(I want to be cremated!)

On our way back we never stopped at all, except at night, because without a moon it was simply too dark to drive. It was raining. There was a gurgling sound all night long, we left our headlamps on, although we were stationary, and there was a rushing of water like the Flood, the earth steamed in front of our headlamps, the rain was lukewarm and heavy. With no wind. What we could see in the cones of the head-lamps was vegetation, motionless, the loops of aerial roots that gleamed in the light from our headlamps like entrails. I was glad not to be alone, although there was really no danger, looking at the situation objectively; the water flowed away. We didn't get a minute's sleep. We squatted there without clothes; it was unbearable to have the wet stuff against our bodies. And yet, as I kept telling myself, it was only water, no reason to feel disgusted. Towards morning the rain stopped, suddenly, like a shower being turned off; but the vegetation still dripped, there was no end to the gurgling and dripping. Then the dawn. It hadn't got any cooler; the morning was hot and steamy, the sun slimy as always, the leaves glistened, and we were wet with sweat and rain and oil, smeary like newborn babies. I was driving; I don't know how we got our Land Rover across the river; but we did get it across; and we couldn't understand how we could ever have swum in this lukewarm water with putrid bubbles. The mud sprayed upon either side when we drove through the pools, those pools in the red of dawn. At one point Marcel said: 'Tu sais que la mort est femme!' I looked at him. 'Et que la terre est femme!' he said, and I could understand the latter, because that's what it looked like, just like that, I laughed out loud, involuntarily, as though at a dirty joke . . .

*

We had only just left port when I saw the girl with the blonde pony-tail for the first time, we had to queue up in the dining-room for our table tickets. I didn't really care who sat at my table, though I hoped it would be one for men only, no matter what language they spoke. But there was no suggestion of choice! The steward had a plan in front of him, a French bureaucrat, ungracious towards those who didn't understand French but loquacious when it suited him, infinitely charming as we waited in a long line. In front of me stood a young girl in black jeans, very little shorter than I, English or Scandinavian I guessed, I couldn't see her face, only her blonde or reddish pony-tail that swung to and fro every time she moved her head. Of course I looked around to see if there was anyone I knew; it might have happened. I really hoped to be put at a table for men only. I only noticed the girl because her pony-tail was dangling in front of my face for at least half an hour. As I have said, I didn't see her face. I tried to guess what it looked like. To pass the time; as people do crossword puzzles to pass the time. Apart from her there were very few young people. She was wearing (I remember it perfectly) a black roll-necked sweater, existentialist, with a necklace of plain wooden beads, rope-soled shoes, everything pretty cheap. She was smoking, she had a thick book under her arm and a green comb protruded from the back pocket of her jeans. It was simply the waiting that forced me to look at her. She must be very young – the down on her neck, her movements, her little ears which went red when the steward made a joke. She merely shrugged her shoulders; she didn't mind whether it was first or second service.

She was put in with the first, I with the second.

Meanwhile the last stretch of the American coast, Long Island, had also disappeared; now there was nothing but water all around us. I took my camera down into the cabin, where I saw my fellow-passenger for the first time, a young man as strong as a tree, Lajser Lewin, an agriculturist from

Israel. I let him have the lower bunk. When I came into the
cabin he was sitting on the upper one, as stated on his ticket;
but I think we both felt better when he sat on the lower bunk
to unpack his belongings. An avalanche of a man! I shaved,
as I hadn't had a chance to do so in the rush that morning. I
plugged in my shaver, the same one as yesterday, and it
worked. Mr Lewin had been studying Californian agriculture. I shaved, without talking much.

Afterwards I went up on deck again.

There was nothing to see, water all around, I stood and
enjoyed being out of reach – instead of getting hold of a deck-
chair.

I didn't know about that sort of thing yet.

Gulls were following the ship.

I couldn't imagine how I was to pass five days on this ship,
I walked up and down with my hands in my trouser pockets,
at one moment pushed by the wind, almost flying along, at
another against the wind, laboriously, so that I had to lean
forward with my trousers flapping. I wondered where the
other passengers got their chairs from. Every chair was
marked with a name. When I asked the steward, there
weren't any deck-chairs left.

Sabeth was playing ping-pong.

She played magnificently, tick-tack, tick-tack, the ball
simply flew this way and that, it was a joy to watch. I hadn't
played myself for years.

She didn't recognize me.

I had nodded ...

She was playing with a young gentleman. Possibly her boy
friend or fiancé. She had changed her clothes and was now
wearing an olive-green corduroy frock with a flared skirt,
which I thought suited her better than her boyish trousers –
assuming it was really the same person!

At all events, the other was nowhere to be found.

In the bar, which I discovered by chance, there wasn't a

soul. In the library there were nothing but novels and elsewhere card tables, which also looked like boredom – outside it was windy, but less boring because at least we were moving.

Really it was only the sun that moved.

Occasionally a cargo boat appeared on the horizon.

At four o'clock tea was served.

Every now and then I stopped by the ping-pong table, surprised every time I saw her from the front, forced to ask myself whether this was really the same person whose face I had tried to guess while we were waiting for our table tickets. I stood by the big window of the promenade deck, smoking and pretending to look out at the sea. Seen from behind, from the reddish pony-tail, it was unquestionably she, but from the front she looked strange. Her eyes were the water-grey that so often goes with red hair. She took off her woolly jacket, because she had lost the game, and rolled up the sleeves of her frock. At one point she almost crashed into me as she ran for the ball. Not a word of apology. The girl didn't even see me.

I moved on.

On deck it turned cold, and even wet, because of the spray, and the steward folded up the chairs. The waves sounded much louder than before, but I could still hear the ping-pong from the floor below, tick-tack, tick-tack. Then the sun went down. I shivered. On my way to the cabin to fetch my overcoat I had to pass through the promenade deck again – I picked up a ball for her, without making a nuisance of myself, I think, she thanked me briefly in English (in general she spoke German) and soon afterwards the gong went for the first service.

I got through the first afternoon.

When I came back with my overcoat and camera to film the sunset, the two ping-pong bats were lying on the green table . . .

*

What difference does it make if I prove that I had no idea, that I couldn't possibly have known? I have destroyed the life of my child and I cannot make restitution. Why draw up a report? I wasn't in love with the girl with the reddish pony-tail, she attracted my attention, that was all, I couldn't have suspected she was my own daughter, I didn't even know I was a father. How does providence come into it? I wasn't in love, on the contrary, she couldn't have seemed more of a stranger once we got into conversation, and it was only through an unlikely coincidence that we got into con-versation at all, my daughter and I. We might just as well have passed one another by. What has providence to do with it? Everything might have turned out quite differently.

*

On the evening of the first day, after I had filmed the sunset, we played ping-pong, our first and last game. Conversation was hardly possible; I had forgotten that anyone could be so young. I explained my camera to her, but everything I said bored her. Our ping-pong went better on my part than I had expected; I hadn't played for decades. Only her service was snappier, it spun. She spun the ball whenever she could, but not always successfully; I kept my end up. Ping-pong is a matter of self-confidence, nothing more. I wasn't as old as the girl thought, and it wasn't quite so much of a pushover as she had obviously expected; I gradually found out how to deal with her shots. I'm sure I bored her. Her opponent of the afternoon, a young man with a toothbrush moustache, nat-urally played a much more impressive game. I was soon red in the face from bending down, but the girl also had to take off her woolly jacket, and even roll up the sleeves of her frock, in order to beat me; she threw back her pony-tail impatiently. As soon as her friend with the moustache appeared and stood watching with a smile on his face and his hands in his pockets, I gave up my bat – she thanked me, but didn't ask me to finish the game, I thanked her, too, and picked up my jacket.

I didn't run after her.

I got into conversation with all kinds of people, particularly Mr Lewin, by no means only with Sabeth, even with the old spinsters at my table, stenographers from Cleveland who felt it their duty to have seen Europe, or with the American clergyman, a Baptist from Chicago, but a jolly fellow.

I'm not used to doing nothing.

Every night before turning in I strolled around all the decks for a breath of air. When I came across her – by chance – arm in arm with her ping-pong friend, she pretended not to notice me; as though I wasn't under any circumstances to know she was in love.

What business was it of mine?

As I said, I was merely going for a breath of air.

She thought I was jealous.

The following morning, while I was standing alone by the rails, she came over to me and asked where my friend was. I wasn't interested in whom she took for my friend, the Israeli agriculturist or the Chicago Baptist, she thought I was feeling lonely and wanted to be kind; she stuck at it until she got me chatting – about navigation, radar, the curvature of the earth, electricity, entropy, which she had never heard of. She was anything but stupid. Not many people to whom I have explained the so-called Maxwell's demon understand as quickly as this young girl, whom I called Sabeth, because Elisabeth seemed to me an impossible name. I liked her, but I didn't flirt with her in the slightest. I feared I must be talking like a teacher, when I saw her smile. Sabeth knew nothing about cybernetics, and as always when you talk to laymen about it, I had to refute all sorts of childish notions about robots, the human resentment towards the machine, which annoys me because it is so short-sighted, and her hackneyed complaint that man isn't a machine. I explained what modern cybernetics means by INFORMATION – our actions or impulses as responses to information, automatic responses that are largely independent of the will, reflexes that a machine can carry out just as well as a man, if not better. Sabeth creased her forehead (as she always did on hearing jokes that she didn't really like) and laughed. I referred her to Norbert Wiener, *Cybernetics or Control and Communication in the Animal and the Machine*, 1948. Of course I wasn't referring to the robots depicted in illustrated papers, but to the lightning calculating machine, also known as the electronic brain, because it is controlled by vacuum electron tubes, a machine that far surpasses any human brain. Two million additions or subtractions a minute! It does an infinitesimal calculus in the same time, it converts logarithms faster than you can read off the result, and a sum that would previously have taken a mathematician his whole life to work out is calculated in a matter of hours and calculated more reliably, because the machine cannot forget anything, because it has a greater power than the human brain to grasp information and assess its probability value. Above all, however, the machine has no feelings, it feels no fear and no hope, which only disturb, it had no wishes with regard to the result, it operates according to the pure logic of probability. For this reason I assert that the robot perceives more accurately than man, it knows more about the future, for it calculates it, it neither speculates nor dreams, but is controlled by its own findings (the feedback) and cannot make mistakes; the robot has no need of intuition ...

Sabeth thought me funny.

Nevertheless, she liked me a little, I believe; anyhow, she nodded when she saw me on deck, she was lying in her deck-chair and immediately picked up her book, but she nodded ...

'Hello, Mr Faber.'

She called me Mr Faber, because I was so used to the English pronunciation of my name that that was how I introduced myself; the rest of the time, we spoke German.

I often left her in peace.

Really I ought to have been working.

A sea voyage is a funny situation. Five days without a car! I'm used to working or driving my car, it's no holiday for me if there's no mechanism running, and in any case anything unusual makes me edgy. I couldn't work. We sailed and sailed, the engines chugged away day and night, I could hear them and feel them, we sailed incessantly, but only the sun moved, or else the moon, the idea that we were sailing along might have been an illusion; however much our tub pitched and threw up waves, the horizon remained the horizon and we remained in the centre of a chalk circle, as though fixed, only the waves slid by, I don't know at how many knots, anyway pretty fast, but nothing changed – except that we grew older!

Sabeth played ping-pong or read.

I roamed about half the day, although it's impossible to meet someone who isn't on board; I hadn't walked so much in ten years as I walked on that ship; sometimes the Baptist joined in the childish game of pushing wooden disks around, just to pass the time, I had more time than ever before and yet I didn't even get around to reading the ship's newspaper.

TODAY'S NEWS ...

Only the sun moved.

PRESIDENT EISENHOWER SAYS ...

I should worry!

The important thing is push your wooden disk into the right square, and it is quite certain that no one can turn up who is not already on board, Ivy for example, one is simply out of reach.

The weather was fine.

One morning, while I was having breakfast with the Baptist, Sabeth sat down at our table, which really pleased me, Sabeth in her jeans. There were plenty of empty tables all around, I mean if the girl couldn't stand me. I was really pleased. They talked about the Louvre in Paris, which I didn't know, and meanwhile I peeled my apple. Her English went splendidly. Again I felt amazed at her youthfulness. At moments like this you wonder whether you were ever that young yourself. The ideas she had! There simply couldn't be such a thing as a man who didn't know the Louvre because it didn't interest him; Sabeth thought I must be pulling her leg. But it was the Baptist who pulled my leg.

'Mr Faber is an engineer,' he said.

What irritated me was not his stupid jokes about engineers, but the way he flirted with the young girl, who hadn't come over to the table on his account, the way he laid his hand on her arm, then on her shoulder, then on her arm again, his fleshy hand. Why did he keep touching the girl all the time? Just because he was an expert on the Louvre.

'Listen,' he kept saying, 'listen.'

Sabeth: 'Yes, I'm listening.'

And yet the Baptist had nothing to say, the sole object of all his talk about the Louvre was an excuse to paw the girl in his old-gentlemanly way, while he poked fun at me.

'Go on,' he said to me, 'go on.'

I took the standpoint that the profession of technologist, a man who masters matter, is a masculine profession, if not the only masculine profession there is. I told them we were on a ship, that is to say a product of technology . . .

'True,' he said, 'very true.'

And all the time he held her arm, pretending to be interested and attentive merely so as not to have to let go of the girl's arm.

'Go on,' he said, 'go on.'

The girl came to my aid. As I hadn't seen the sculptures in the Louvre she brought the conversation around to my robots; but I didn't feel like talking about them and merely said that sculptures and things like that are nothing more (to my way of thinking) than forbears of the robot. Primitive peoples tried to annul death by portraying the human body – we do it by finding substitutes for the human body. Technology instead of mysticism!

Fortunately Mr Lewin joined us.

When it turned out that Mr Lewin had never been to the Louvre either, the conversation changed, thank goodness. Mr Lewin had been over the engine-room the day before. This led to a split in the conversation: the Baptist and Sabeth went on talking about Van Gogh, Lewin and I discussed diesel engines, during which time I, though interested in diesel engines, did not take my eyes off the girl. She listened attentively to the Baptist while she took his hand and laid it down beside her like a table napkin.

'Why do you laugh?' he asked me.

I was simply laughing.

'Van Gogh was the most intelligent fellow of his time,' he told me. 'Have you ever read his letters?'

Sabeth added: 'He really knows a lot.'

But as soon as Mr Lewin and I started talking about electricity, our Baptist and cock of the walk didn't know anything any more, but sat peeling his apple without a word.

Eventually we discussed Israel.

Afterwards, on deck, Sabeth (without any pressure from me) expressed the wish to look over the engine-room – with me; I had merely said I intended to look over the engine-room too some time. I didn't want to be a nuisance to her. She wondered why I hadn't got a deck-chair and immediately offered me hers, because anyhow she had a ping-pong date.

I thanked her and she was gone.

After that I often sat in her deck-chair, the steward used to get her chair out the moment he saw me, open it up and greet me as Mr Piper, because her chair was labelled MISS E. PIPER.

I told myself that probably every young girl would somehow remind me of Hanna. I had begun to think a great deal about Hanna again lately. Where was the likeness? Hanna had black hair, Sabeth reddish blonde, and it seemed to me very far-fetched to compare the two of them. I did it out of sheer idleness. Sabeth was young, as young as Hanna had been in those days, and moreover she spoke the same High German, but after all (I told myself) there are whole ethnic groups that speak High German. I lay for hours in her deckchair with my legs on the rails which trembled, gazing out to sea. Unfortunately I had no engineering periodicals with me and I can't read novels; I preferred to ponder over the problem of what caused this vibration and why it couldn't be eliminated, or else I calculated Hanna's present age and wondered whether her hair would already be white. I closed my eyes to sleep. If Hanna had been on deck I should have recognized her at once, no doubt about it. Perhaps she is on deck! I thought. And I got up and wandered around among the deckchairs, without seriously believing Hanna was really on deck. It was just to pass the time. All the same (I admit) I was afraid she might be there, and I calmly studied all the ladies who were no longer young girls. You can do that when you're wearing dark glasses; you stand smoking and studying people, unnoticed by those you are studying, quite calmly, quite objectively. I estimated their ages, which wasn't at all easy; I paid less attention to the colour of their hair than to their legs and feet, in so far as they were uncovered, and noticed especially their hands and lips. Here and there, I came across full and rosy lips accompanied by a throat that recalled the folded skin of lizards, and I could imagine that Hanna was still very beautiful, I mean lovable. Unfortunately I couldn't see their eyes, because of the sun glasses. All sorts of worn-out goods lay there, all sorts of organisms that had probably never blossomed. American women, the products of cosmetics. I knew Hanna would never look like that.

I sat down again.

The wind whistled in the funnel.

The waves frothed and foamed.

Once a cargo boat appeared on the horizon.

I was bored, hence all this musing about Hanna; I lay with my legs resting on the white railing that never stopped vibrating, and what I knew about Hanna was just enough for the description of a wanted person that would be no use if the person wasn't there. I couldn't see her, not even with my eyes shut.

Twenty years is a long time.

Instead (I opened my eyes, because someone had bumped into my chair) I saw again the young thing called Fräulein Elisabeth Piper.

She had finished playing ping-pong.

What struck me most was the way she threw back her pony-tail to emphasize her disagreement in conversation (and yet Hanna never wore a pony-tail), or the way she shrugged her shoulders when it really wasn't a matter of indifference to her, simply out of pride. But above all it was the small, brief wrinkling of her forehead between the eyebrows, when I made a joke at which she had to laugh but really thought stupid. It struck me, it occupied my mind. I liked it. There are gestures you like, because you have seen them somewhere or other before. I am always sceptical when people talk about a likeness; from experience. How often my brother and I used to laugh ourselves silly, when good people, with no idea of the facts, remarked on our striking resemblance! My brother was adopted. When anyone (for example) puts his right hand around the back of his head to scratch his left temple, it catches my attention, I immediately think of my father, but it would never occur to me to take someone for my father's

85

brother merely because he scratched himself like this. I believe in reason. I'm no Baptist or spiritualist. How could I guess that a girl called Elisabeth Piper was Hanna's daughter? If I had the slightest suspicion on the ship (or later) that there might be any real connection between the young girl and Hanna, who was understandably on my mind after the business with Joachim, of course I should immediately have asked: Who is her mother? What is her name? Where does she come from? I don't know how I should have acted, but anyhow differently, that's obvious, I'm not pathological, I should have treated my daughter as my daughter, I'm not a pervert!

It was all so natural.

A harmless shipboard friendship.

Once Sabeth was rather seasick; instead of going up on deck, as she was advised, she insisted on going to her cabin, then she was sick in the corridor, her friend with the moustache laid her on her bunk, as if he was her husband. Fortunately I was there. Sabeth in her black jeans, with her face turned to one side on account of her pony-tail, lay a limp heap with her legs spread out and her face as pale as china clay. He held her hand. I immediately unscrewed a port-hole to let more air in, and fetched water.

'Thanks,' he said, as he sat on the edge of her bunk; then he unlaced her rope-soled shoes, playing the Good Samaritan. As though her sickness came from her feet!

I stayed in the cabin.

Her red belt was far too tight, you could see that, but I didn't think it was our business to loosen the belt . . .

I introduced myself.

We had no sooner shaken hands than he sat down on the edge of her bunk again. Perhaps he was really her boy friend, Sabeth was already a proper woman, when she lay like that, not a child; I took a blanket from the upper bunk, in case she was cold, and covered her up.

86

'Thank you,' he said.

I was simply waiting till the young man also felt there was no more to be done and that it would be better to leave the girl by herself now.

'*Ciao!*' he said.

I saw through him, he wanted to lose me on deck somewhere and then go back to her cabin alone. I challenged him to a game of ping-pong. ... He wasn't as stupid as I had expected, though I didn't take to him at all. Why do people grow moustaches? We couldn't play ping-pong, because both the tables were occupied again; instead I got him involved in a conversation – in High German, of course! – about turbines; he was an illustrator by profession, an artist, but businesslike. As soon as he saw that painting and the theatre and that sort of thing cut no ice with me, he talked in business terms, not unscrupulous, but businesslike, a Swiss, as it turned out . . .

I don't know what Sabeth saw in him.

There was no reason for feelings of inferiority on my part. I'm no genius, but all the same I have an important position, only I find it less and less easy to put up with these young people, their way of talking, their genius, though all the time they have nothing but dreams of the future to preen themselves about; they don't give a damn for what we have already achieved in this world; if you tell them, they just smile politely.

'I don't want to keep you,' I said.

'Will you excuse me?'

'Of course,' I said . . .

When I brought the tablets that had helped me, Sabeth wouldn't let anyone into her cabin. It was funny, because she was dressed, as I could see through the crack of the door. I had promised her the tablets earlier on, that was the only reason I came. She took the tablets through the crack of the door. I don't know whether he was in the cabin. I begged the

87

girl really to take the tablets. I only wanted to help her; for holding hands and taking off her shoes hadn't helped her. I really wasn't interested in whether a girl like Sabeth (her lack of inhibitions always puzzled me) had been with a man yet or not. I merely wondered.

What I knew at the time was this:

A year at Yale on a scholarship, now on her way home to mother, who lived in Athens, Herr Piper, on the other hand, in East Germany because he still believed in Communism, her main concern at the moment to find a cheap hotel in Paris – then she wanted to hitchhike to Rome (which I thought crazy) and didn't know what she was going to be, a pediatrician or an industrial designer or something like that, or perhaps an air hostess so that she could fly a lot, and whatever happened she wanted to see India and China. Sabeth (in response to my inquiry) guessed my age at forty, but when I told her I was just on fifty she showed no surprise. She was twenty. What impressed her most about me was the fact that I could personally remember Lindbergh's first flight over the Atlantic in 1927, when I was twenty. She had to work it out before she would believe me. At my age, as seen by Sabeth, I don't think it would have made any difference if I had talked in the same tone about Napoleon. I generally stood at the rail, because I couldn't let Sabeth (who was generally in a bathing costume) sit on the floor, while I lay in the chair; that was too avuncular for my liking. On the other hand, it would also have been funny if Sabeth lay in the chair while I sat beside her with my legs crossed . . .

In no case did I want to impose myself on her.

I played chess with Mr Lewin, whose mind was on agriculture, or with other passengers who were checkmated after twenty moves at most; it was boring, but I preferred boring myself to boring the girl! What I mean is, I only went to Sabeth when I could really think of something to say.

I forbade her to become an air hostess.

Sabeth was generally absorbed in her thick book, and when she talked about Tolstoy I really wondered what a girl like that actually knew about men. I don't know Tolstoy. Of course she was teasing me when she said:

'Now you're talking like Tolstoy again!'

And yet she admired Tolstoy.

Once, in the bar, I suddenly told her – I don't know why – about my friend who couldn't stick it, and how we found him: fortunately behind closed windows, otherwise the zopilotes would have torn him in shreds like a dead donkey.

Sabeth thought I was exaggerating.

I drank my third or fourth Pernod, laughed and told her what a man looks like hanging on a wire – both feet off the ground, as though he could fly . . .

The chair had fallen over.

He had a beard.

I don't know why I told her all this, Sabeth thought me cynical, because I couldn't help laughing; but he was really as stiff as a doll . . .

I was also smoking a great deal.

His face was black with blood.

He rotated like a scarecrow in the wind.

Moreover he stank.

His finger-nails were purple, his arms grey, his hands whitish, the colour of sponges . . .

I didn't recognize him.

His tongue was also bluish . . .

There was really nothing to tell, it was simply an accident, he rotated in the warm wind, as I have said, the part above the wire was bloated . . .

I didn't want to talk about it at all.

His arms were as stiff as two stakes . . .

Unfortunately my Guatemala films hadn't been developed yet, you can't describe it, you have to see what a man looks like dangling at the end of a wire.

Sabeth in her blue evening frock . . .

At times I suddenly saw my friend hanging before my eyes, as though we hadn't buried him, all of a sudden – perhaps because there was a radio playing in this bar too, he hadn't even switched off his radio.

That's how it was.

When we found him, as I have said, his radio was on. Not loud. At first we thought somebody was speaking in the room above, but there wasn't any room above, my friend lived quite alone, and when the voice was followed by music we realized it must be the radio and of course we turned it off, because it was unsuitable, because it was dance music . . .

Sabeth asked questions.

Why did he do it?

He didn't tell us, he just hung there like a doll and stank and rotated in the warm wind . . .

That's how it was.

When I stood up I knocked over my chair, there was a crash, people looked round, but the girl picked my chair up as though nothing had happened and wanted to take me to my cabin, but I didn't want to go there.

I wanted to go on deck.

I wanted to be alone . . .

I was drunk.

If I had mentioned his name, Joachim Hencke, everything would have come to light. Evidently I didn't even mention his first name, but simply talked about a friend who hanged himself in Guatemala, about a tragic accident.

Once I filmed her.

When Sabeth finally noticed, she put her tongue out; I filmed her with her tongue out, until, really angry, she bawled me out properly. 'What's the big idea?' she asked me straight out: 'What do you want with me anyway?'

That was in the morning.

I should have asked Sabeth if she was a Moslem, or had

some other superstitious fear of being filmed. The impudence of the girl! I was perfectly willing to take the film (together with the telescopic shots of Ivy waving) out of the camera and ruin it by holding it up to the sun. What angered me most was the tone of voice in which she said:

'You keep watching me all the time, Mr Faber, I don't like it.'

This remark kept ringing in my ears all the morning, and I wondered what the girl took me for when she made it.

She didn't like me.

That much was obvious, and any illusions I might have had were dissipated later when, soon after lunch, I reminded her of my promise to tell her when I was going to look over the engine-room.

'Now?' she asked.

She had to finish a chapter.

'Very well,' she said.

I wrote her off. Without feeling offended. I've always taken it that way; I don't like myself when I'm a burden to other people, and it's never been my practice to run after women who don't like me; frankly, I never needed to . . .

The engine-room of a ship like this is as big as a fair-sized factory; the major element is the big diesel power unit and besides this there are the generating, warm-water and ventilating plant. Although there was nothing out of the ordinary for even the expert to see, I nevertheless found the installation as such, conditioned as it was by the shape of the hull, worth looking at, quite apart from the fact that it is always a pleasure to watch machinery in operation. I explained the main control panel, without going into details; I explained briefly what a kilowatt is, what hydraulics is, what an ampère is, things Sabeth had learnt at school and forgotten, of course, but she had no difficulty in understanding them again now. What impressed her most were all the pipes, never mind what they were for, and the great stair-shaft with a view up through five or six floors to the sky behind a criss-cross of iron bars. She was worried by the fact that the engine-room crew, all of whom she thought so friendly, sweated all the time and spent their whole lives on the ocean without seeing the ocean. I noticed how they stared when the girl (whom they obviously took for my daughter) clambered from one iron ladder to another.

Ça va, mademoiselle, ça va?'

Sabeth climbed like a cat.

'Pas trop vite, ma petite . . .'

I found their male grimaces impertinent, but Sabeth noticed none of all this, Sabeth in her black jeans with the once white seams, the green comb in her back pocket, the reddish pony-tail dangling over her back, the two shoulder blades under her black pullover, the groove in her taut, slim back, then her hips, her youthful thighs in the black trousers that were crumpled at the calves, her ankles – I found her beautiful, but not provocative. Just very beautiful. We were standing at the glass peephole of a diesel burner, which I explained briefly, my hands in my trouser pockets to avoid taking hold of her near arm or shoulder as the Baptist had done at breakfast.

I didn't want to touch the girl.

I suddenly felt very senile.

I took hold of both her hips as her foot sought in vain for the lowest rung of an iron ladder, and lifted her straight down on to the floor. Her hips were remarkably light and at the same time strong, gripping them was like gripping the steering wheel of my Studebaker, the same slenderness, exactly the same diameter – just for a second, then she was standing on the landing of perforated sheet metal; she didn't blush in the least, but thanked me for my unnecessary help and wiped her hands on a bundle of brightly coloured cotton waste. I hadn't felt stirred by the contact either, and we walked on to the big propeller shafts, which I wanted to show her before we went back on deck. Problems of torsion, index of friction, fatigue of the steel through vibration and so on, I only thought of these things in my own mind, amidst a noise so loud you could scarcely speak – I merely explained to the girl where we were; namely at the point where the propeller shafts leave the hull to drive the screws outside. We had to shout. We must have been roughly twenty-five feet below sea level. I said I would inquire. 'Roughly,' I shouted. 'It might be only twenty feet.' I pointed out the considerable pressure of water this structure had to stand up to. This was too technical again – her childish imagination was already outside with the fishes, while I was still discussing shipbuilding. 'Here,' I shouted taking her hand and placing it on the two and three-quarter inch rivets, so that she could understand what I was talking about. 'Sharks?' That was the only word I caught. 'What do you mean, sharks!' I shouted back. 'I've no idea.' I continued to talk about the construction of the ship. Her eyes were staring.

I had wanted to give her something.

Our voyage was drawing to an end, I thought it a pity, suddenly the last little thread on the chart of the Atlantic, a remnant of three inches – an afternoon and a night and a morning . . .

Mr Lewin was already packing.

We discussed tipping.

When I pictured how we should all be saying good bye in twenty-four hours, good-bye with humorous good wishes on all sides – Mr Lewin, best of luck in agriculture! And our Baptist, best of luck in the Louvre! And the girl with the reddish ponytail and the indeterminate future, best of luck – I was troubled by the thought that we should never hear of one another again.

I sat in the bar.

Shipboard friendships!

I grew sentimental, which wasn't like me, and there was a

big dance, which was evidently the usual thing, this was the last evening on board and it happened to be my fiftieth birthday; naturally, I didn't mention this.

It was my first offer of marriage.

I was really sitting with Mr Lewin, who didn't care for dancing either; I had invited him to a burgundy, the best thing to be had on board (you're only fifty once, I thought): Beaune 1933, a magnificent bouquet, a bit lacking in flavour, too brief, and unfortunately a trifle cloudy, which didn't worry Mr Lewin, who even enjoyed Californian burgundy. I was disappointed (I had pictured my fiftieth birthday rather differently, to be frank) with the wine, but otherwise quite contented, Sabeth just joined us for a moment every now and then to take a sip from her *citron pressé*, then along came another dancing partner, her illustrator with the moustache, and in between ship's officers in dress uniform, as spick and span as in an operetta, Sabeth in her unchanging blue evening frock, not in bad taste, but cheap, too childish . . . I wondered whether to go to bed, I could feel my stomach, and we were sitting too near the orchestra, there was an infernal din and on top of it this tumultuous carnival wherever you looked – Chinese lanterns, blurred in the haze from cigarettes and cigars like the sun over Guatemala, streamers, paper chains everywhere, a jungle of red and green frippery, gentlemen in dinner jackets, as black as zopilotes, whose plumage gleams in just the same way . . .

I didn't want to think of that.

The day after tomorrow in Paris – that was about all I could think of in this racket – I would go to a doctor and have my stomach examined at last.

It was a queer evening.

Mr Lewin, the gigantic fellow, grew positively witty, being unused to wine, and suddenly gained the courage to dance with Sabeth; she came up to his ribs, while he had to duck his head to avoid getting tangled up in streamers. Mr Lewin didn't possess a dark suit and danced a mazurka to everything, because he was born in Poland and had spent his childhood in the Ghetto and so on. Sabeth had to stretch up in order to take him by the shoulders, like a schoolgirl straphanging in the underground. I sat swilling the burgundy around in my glass, determined not to get sentimental because it was my birthday, and drinking. All the Germans on board were drinking champagne; I couldn't help thinking of Herbert and the future of the German cigar, and wondering what Herbert could be doing all alone among the Indians.

Later I went up on deck.

I was completely sober, and when Sabeth came and joined me I said straight away that she would catch cold in her thin evening frock. She wanted to know whether I was melancholy. Because I wasn't dancing. I think they're fun, their modern dances, existentialist jigs, in which everyone dances on his own, cuts his own capers, tangled up in his own legs, shivering as though with the ague, all rather epileptic, but fun, full of go, I must admit, but I can't do it.

Why should I be melancholy?

England wasn't in sight yet.

When I gave her my jacket so that she shouldn't catch cold, her pony-tail simply wouldn't stay at the back of her head, the wind was blowing so hard.

The red funnels gleamed in the searchlight.

Sabeth thought it 'dandy', a night like this on deck, with the wind whistling through the ropes and flapping the canvas covers on the lifeboats and blowing the smoke from the funnels.

The music was almost inaudible.

We talked about constellations – the usual thing, when two people haven't yet discovered which one knows less about the stars than the other; the rest is romantic fantasy, which I can't bear. I showed her the comet which was visible at that time in the north. I was within an ace of telling her it was my birthday. Hence the comet! But it wasn't even true as a joke; the comet had been visible for several weeks already, though never so clearly as on that night, from at least 26 April. So I didn't say anything about my birthday, 29 April.

'I've got two wishes,' I said, 'now that we're saying goodbye. First, that you shouldn't become an air hostess . . .'

'And second?'

'Second,' I said, 'that you shouldn't hitchhike to Rome. Seriously. I'd rather pay your fare by rail or plane . . .'

At the time I never thought for a moment that we should be driving to Rome together, Sabeth and I, since I really had no reason for going to Rome.

She laughed in my face.

She misunderstood me.

After midnight there was a cold buffet, as usual – I pretended I was hungry and took Sabeth below, because she was shivering, as I could see, in spite of my jacket. Her chin was shivering.

Down below they were still dancing.

Her supposition that I was melancholy because I was alone put me out of humour. I'm used to travelling alone. I live, like every real man, in my work. On the contrary, that's the way I like it and I think myself lucky to live alone, in my view this is the only possible condition for men, I enjoy waking up and not having to say a word. Where is the woman who can understand that? Even the inquiry as to how I have slept vexes me, because my thoughts are already beyond that, I'm used to thinking ahead, not backwards, I'm used to planning. Caresses in the evening, yes, but I can't stand caresses in the morning, and frankly more than three or four days with one woman has always been for me the beginning of dissimulation, no man can stand feelings in the morning. I'd rather wash dishes!

Sabeth laughed.

96

Breakfast with women, yes, as an exception while on holiday, breakfast on a balcony, but frankly I have never been
able to stand it for longer than three weeks, it's all right on
holiday, when you don't know what to do with the whole
day anyhow, but after three weeks (at the latest) I long for
turbines; a woman with time on her hands in the morning, a
woman who wanders about before she is dressed, for
example, rearranging flowers in a vase and talking about love
and marriage, is something no man can stand, I believe,
unless he dissembles. I couldn't help thinking of Ivy. As far
as I am concerned every woman is like clinging ivy. I want to
be alone. The very sight of a double room, unless it's in
a hotel I can leave again soon, a double room as a perman-
ent arrangement, sets me thinking about the Foreign
Legion ...

Sabeth thought me cynical.

But I was only telling the truth.

I stopped talking, although I don't think Mr Lewin understood a word; he put his hand over the glass when I went to fill
it up, and Sabeth, who thought me cynical, was fetched away
to dance .... I'm not cynical. I'm merely realistic, which is
something women can't stand. I'm not a monster, as Ivy said,
and I have nothing against marriage in principle; as a rule the
women themselves considered I wasn't suited to it. I can't
have feelings all the time. Being alone is the only possible
condition for me, since I don't want to make a woman unhappy, and women have a tendency to become unhappy.
Being alone isn't always fun, you can't always be in form.
Moreover, I have learned from experience that once you're
not in form women don't remain in form either; as soon as
they're bored they start complaining you've no feelings.
Then, to be quite frank, I'd rather be bored on my own. I
admit that I'm not always in the mood for television either
(although, by the way, I am convinced that television will
become even better in the next few years) and am sometimes

T–HF–D

prey to low spirits, but then especially I'm glad to be alone. One of the happiest moments I know is the moment when I have left a party, when I get into my car, shut the door and insert the ignition key, switch on, turn on the radio, light my cigarette with the built-in lighter and put my foot down; people are a strain as far as I'm concerned, even men. As to my fluctuating spirits, I pay no attention to them. Sometimes you feel low, but you pick up again. Fatigue phenomena! As in steel. Feelings, I have observed, are fatigue phenomena, that's all, at any rate in my case. You get run down. Then writing letters doesn't help you to feel less lonely either. It doesn't make any difference; afterwards you still hear your own footsteps in the empty flat. The radio announcers boosting dog food, baking powder or what have you, and then suddenly falling silent after wishing you good-bye 'till tomorrow morning at 6 o'clock'. And now it's only two o'clock. Then gin, although I don't like gin on its own, in the background voices from the street, cars hooting or the rumble of the underground trains, every now and then the roar of an aeroplane, sounds like that. Sometimes I just fall asleep, the newspaper on my lap and my cigarette on the carpet. I pull myself together. What for? Somewhere there is a late broadcast with symphonies, which I switch off. What else? Then I just stand there with gin, which I don't like, in my glass, drinking; I stand still so as not to hear steps in my flat, steps that are after all only my own. The whole thing isn't tragic, merely wearisome. You can't wish yourself good night . . .

Is that a reason for marrying?

Sabeth, when she came back from her dance to drink her *citron pressé*, snubbed me. Mr Lewin, the gigantic fellow, was asleep, smiling as though he could see the whole carnival even in his sleep, the streamers and the couples busily engaged in bursting one another's balloons.

She asked what I was thinking all the time.

I didn't know.

I asked what she was thinking.

She knew at once:

'You ought to get married, Mr Faber.'

Then her friend turned up again, after hunting for her all over the ship, to ask her for a dance. He looked at me.

'Please go ahead,' I said.

I only kept her handbag.

I knew exactly what I was thinking. There were no words for it. I swilled the wine round in my glass in order to smell it and tried not to think of the way men and women couple, in spite of the picture that sprang unbidden to my mind accompanied by a feeling of amazement and the sudden shock that jerks you out of a doze. Why just like that? Looking at it from the outside, why just with the abdomen? When you sit watching dancers and visualize it with complete detachment, it doesn't seem humanly possible. Why just like that? It's absurd, when you're not impelled to it yourself by your instincts, it makes you feel you must be crazy even to have such an idea, positively perverse.

I ordered beer . . .

Perhaps the fault is in me.

The couples, incidentally, were in the process of dancing with an orange held between their noses . . .

What is it like for Lajser Lewin?

He was actually snoring, I couldn't speak to him; his half-open mouth looked like the red mouth of a fish against the green aquarium glass.

I thought about Ivy.

Of Ivy when I embraced her and thought to myself, I must get my films developed, or ring up Williams. I could have solved a chess problem in my head, while Ivy was saying, I'm happy, oh dear, so happy, oh dear, oh dear! I felt her ten fingers round the back of my head, I saw her epileptically happy mouth and the picture on the wall that was crooked again, I wondered what the date was today, I heard her ask,

Are you happy? and I closed my eyes in order to think about Ivy, whom I was holding in my arms, and I accidentally kissed my own elbow. Afterwards everything seems forgotten. I forgot to ring Williams, although I had been thinking about it all the time. I stood by the open window smoking my cigarette at last, while Ivy made tea outside, and I suddenly knew the date. But it didn't make any difference what the date was. Everything was as though it had never happened. Then I heard someone come into the room and turned round, and it was Ivy in her dressing gown bringing our cups, and I went up to her and said Ivy! and kissed her, because she was a good kid, although she couldn't understand that I would rather be alone . . .

Suddenly our ship came to a stop.

Mr Lewin, suddenly awake, although I hadn't said a word, wanted to know whether we had reached Southampton.

There were lights outside.

It was probably Southampton.

Mr Lewin stood up and went on deck.

I drank my beer and tried to remember whether it also used to be absurd with Hanna (in the old days), whether it had always been absurd.

Everyone went on deck.

When Sabeth came back into the festooned hall to fetch her handbag, I got a surprise: she dismissed her friend, who made a sour face, and sat down beside me. Her Hanna-as-a-girl face! She asked me for a cigarette and wanted to know once again what I was pondering about all the time. I had to say something, I gave her a light, which illumined her young face, and asked whether she would marry me.

Sabeth blushed.

Was I serious?

Why not?

Outside they were unloading the cargo, and everyone felt he ought to watch it; the weather was cold, but this was a point of honour, the ladies were shivering in their evening dresses, there was mist, a night full of lights, gentlemen in dinner jackets who tried to warm their ladies with embraces, searchlights that lit up the hold, gentlemen in paper hats, the noise of cranes, but all in the mist; the flashing lights on shore . . .

We stood without touching.

I had said what I never meant to say, but what has been said cannot be unsaid, I enjoyed our silence, I was completely sober again, but all the same I had no idea what I was thinking, probably nothing.

My life was in her hands . . .

For a time, Mr Lewin came between us; he wasn't in the way, on the contrary, I think Sabeth and I were both glad, we stood arm in arm chatting with Mr Lewin, who had slept off his burgundy, discussing the problem of tips and so on. Our ship had been riding at anchor for at least an hour, day was already breaking. Then we were alone again, the last people left on the wet deck, and Sabeth asked me whether I meant it seriously. I kissed her on the forehead, and then on her cold and trembling eyelids, she was shivering all over, then on her mouth, which gave me a fright. She was more of a stranger than any other girl. Her parted lips – it was impossible. I kissed the wet tears from her eye sockets, there was nothing to be said, it was impossible.

In another day and a half we entered Le Havre.

It was raining, and I was standing on the upper deck, when the young stranger with the reddish pony-tail crossed the bridge carrying luggage in both hands, which prevented her from waving. I think she saw me wave. I had meant to take a film, I went on waving, although I couldn't see her in the crush. Later in the customs shed, just as I had to open my trunk, I caught sight of her reddish pony-tail once more; she nodded too and smiled, both hands full of luggage, she was carrying far too much, to save herself a porter, but I couldn't help her, she vanished into the throng – our child! But I couldn't know that at the time, nevertheless I felt a strangling sensation in my throat as I saw her simply disappear in the crowd. I was fond of her. That was all I knew. On the boat train to Paris I could have gone through all the compartments again. What for? We had said good-bye.

In Paris I immediately phoned Williams, to give a preliminary oral report; he said hello and had no time to listen to my explanation. I wondered whether anything was wrong ... Paris was the usual thing, a week filled with conferences. I was staying on the Quai Voltaire as usual and had my customary room looking out on to the Seine and this Louvre, which I had never visited though it stood right opposite.

Williams was odd.

'That's okay,' he kept saying, 'That's okay,' all the time I was accounting for my short trip to Guatemala, which, as it turned out when I reached Caracas, had not caused any delay, since our turbines were not yet ready for assembly, quite apart from the fact that I had arrived in time for this conference here in Paris, which was the most important event of the month. 'That's okay,' he said again when I told him about the ghastly suicide of the friend of my youth. 'That's okay,' and finally he said: 'What about taking a holiday, Walter?'

I couldn't understand what he meant.

'What about taking a holiday?' he said. 'You look as though ...'

We were interrupted.

'This is Mr Faber. This is ...'

I don't know whether Williams was annoyed because I hadn't come by plane, but had taken a ship for a change; his suggestion that I needed a holiday could only be intended ironically, for I have seldom been as sun-tanned as I was then, and after all the good food on board I was less gaunt than usual, and sun-tanned on top of that ...

Williams was odd.

Later, after the conference, I went to a restaurant I didn't know, alone and depressed every time I thought of Williams. He wasn't generally petty. Did he by any chance imagine I'd had a bit of a love affair in Guatemala or somewhere else *en route*? His smile vexed me, because in professional matters, as I have said, I am conscientiousness personified; I have never – as Williams very well knew – been as much as half an hour late for a conference on account of a woman. That just didn't happen with me. But more than anything else I was vexed because the distrust or whatever it was, expressed in his repeated remarks of 'That's okay', so preoccupied me that the waiter also treated me as though I was an idiot.

'*Beaune, monsieur, c'est un vin rouge.*'

'That's okay,' I said.

'*Du vin rouge,*' he said, '*du vin rouge, avec du poisson?*'

I had simply forgotten what I had ordered, my mind was elsewhere; that was no reason to go as red in the face as a beetroot – I was furious at the extent to which this waiter (who behaved as though he were serving a barbarian) sapped my self-confidence. After all, I had no reason to feel inferior, I did my job, I had no ambition to be an inventor, but I did as much, I thought, as any old Baptist from Ohio who poked fun at engineers; what a man like myself achieves is a great deal more useful, I supervise plant that runs into millions, I have whole power stations under me, I've worked in Persia and in Africa (Liberia) and Panama, Venezuela and Peru, I'm no country bumpkin – as this waiter obviously thought.

'*Voilà, monsieur!*'

What a palaver they make when they show you the bottle, uncork it, pour out a trial sip and ask:

'*Il est bon?*'

I hate feeling inferior.

'That's okay,' I said, refusing to be browbeaten, I was well aware that it tasted corked but I didn't want to start an argument. 'That's okay.'

My mind was elsewhere.

I was the only diner, because it was early in the evening; the only thing that irritated me was the mirror facing me, a mirror in a gilt frame. Every time I looked up I saw myself looking like a portrait of one of my own ancestors: Walter Faber, eating salad, in a gilt frame. I had rings under my eyes, that was all, apart from that I was sun-tanned, as I have said, not nearly so gaunt as usual, on the contrary I looked splendid. I'm a man in the prime of life (I knew that without a mirror), grey-haired, but athletic. I've no regard for handsome men. During puberty I used to be worried about the length of my nose, but not since then; since then there have been enough women to free me from false feelings of inferiority: the only thing that irritated me was this restaurant, with its mirrors wherever I looked, and this eternal waiting for my fish. I called firmly for the waiter, I had plenty of time, but what upset me was the feeling that the waiter was treating me with disrespect for some reason, the whole empty restaurant with five whispering waiters and a single diner – Walter Faber crumbling bread in a gilt frame wherever I looked. My fish when it finally arrived, was excellent, but I didn't enjoy it at all, I don't know what was the matter with me.

'You look as though . . .'

It was only this stupid remark of Williams's (and yet he likes me, I know) that made me neglect the fish and keep looking at those ridiculous mirrors that showed eight versions of Walter Faber.

Of course one grows older.

Of course one's hair starts getting thin on top.

I'm not in the habit of going to doctors, I've never been ill in my life, apart from my appendix – I looked at the mirror merely because Williams had said, 'What about taking a holiday, Walter?' And yet I had seldom been so sun-tanned. In the eyes of a young girl, who wanted to become an air hostess, I was a man at the age of discretion perhaps, but not one who had lost interest in life, on the contrary, I forgot to go to a doctor in Paris, as I had actually decided to do . . .

I felt perfectly normal.

The next day (Sunday) I went to the Louvre, but there was no sign of a girl with a reddish pony-tail, although I spent a whole hour in this Louvre.

*

I've really forgotten my first experience with a woman, the very first, that is to say I never remember it at all if I don't want to. She was the wife of a teacher of mine, who used to invite me to his house for week-ends shortly before I took my final examination; I used to help him read the proofs of a new edition of his textbook, in order to earn some money. My dearest wish was a cheap second-hand motorcycle, it didn't matter how old the machine was so long as it went. I had to draw geometrical figures, Pythagoras's theorem and so on, in Indian ink, because I was the best pupil at mathematics and geometry. His wife, as she appeared to me at the age I was then, was a lady in the years of discretion, forty, I believe, consumptive, and when she kissed my boyish body she seemed to me like a madwoman or a bitch; and I continued to address her as 'Frau Professor'. That was absurd. I forgot about it from time to time; only when my teacher came into the classroom and put the exercise books down on the desk without a word, I was afraid he had found out about it, and the whole world would find out about it. As a rule, I was the first he called up when the exercise books were distributed, and I had to go out in front of the class – the only one who had made no mistakes. She died the same summer and I forgot about it, as you forget water you drank somewhere when you were thirsty. Naturally I felt bad about forgetting it and once a month I forced myself to visit her grave; I took a few flowers out of my briefcase, when no one was looking, and quickly placed them on the grave, which had no tombstone yet, only a number; at the same time, I felt ashamed because I was always glad when it was over.

Only with Hanna was it never absurd.

*

It was spring, but it was snowing, as we sat in the Tuileries, flurries of snow descending from a blue sky; we hadn't seen each other for almost a week and she was glad to see me, I thought, because of the cigarettes, she was broke.

'I didn't believe you anyway,' she said, 'when you told me you never went to the Louvre . . .'

'Well, very seldom.'

'Seldom!' she laughed. 'I saw you the day before yesterday already – down there among the antiques – and again yesterday.'

She was really a child, although a chain smoker, she thought it was really coincidence that we had met again in Paris. She was wearing her black jeans and rope-soled shoes again, and with them a duffle coat and no hat, of course, only her reddish pony-tail, and it was snowing, as I have said, out of the blue, so to speak.

'Aren't you cold?'

'No,' she said, 'but you must be.'

I had another conference at 4 p.m.

'Shall we have a coffee?' I said.

'Oh yes,' she said, 'I'd like one.'

As we crossed the Place de la Concorde, hounded by the gendarme's whistle, she gave me her arm. I hadn't expected that. We had to run, because the gendarme had already raised his white bâton and a pack of cars was starting out after us; on the pavement, having escaped arm in arm, I noticed I had lost my hat – it was lying in the middle of the road, already squashed to a brown pulp by a tyre. 'Eh bien!' I said and walked on arm in arm with the girl, hatless like a boy in the flurrying snow.

Sabeth was hungry.

To avoid flattering and deluding myself I decided that she was glad to see me because she had almost no money left; she was stuffing herself with *pâtisserie* so eagerly she could scarcely look up, scarcely speak ... It was impossible to talk her out of her plan to hitchhike to Rome. She had worked out an exact itinerary: she could miss Avignon, Nîmes and Marseilles, but she mustn't miss Pisa, Florence, Siena, Orvieto, Assisi, and what have you; she had tried that morning already, but evidently on the wrong road out of Paris.

'Does your mother know about it?'

She told me she did.

'Doesn't your mother worry?'

The only reason I was still sitting there was because I had to pay, I was all ready to go, with my briefcase resting on my knee; I didn't want to be late just now, when Williams was behaving so oddly.

'Of course she worries,' said the girl, scraping the last remnants of her *pâtisserie* together with her spoon and only prevented by her upbringing from actually licking the plate; then she laughed. 'Mother is always worrying ...'

Later she said:

'I had to promise her I wouldn't go with any Tom, Dick or Harry – but that's obvious, I'm not stupid.'

In the meantime I had paid.

'Thank you,' she said.

I didn't dare ask: what are you doing this evening? I knew less and less what kind of a girl she really was. Uninhibited in what sense? Perhaps she really accepted invitations from any man, an idea that didn't shock me, but which made me jealous, positively sentimental.

'Do you think we shall meet again?' I asked and immediately added: 'If not, I wish you all the best.'

I really had to go.

'Are you going to stay here?'

'Yes,' she said. 'I've got plenty of time.'

'If you've got time to do me a favour . . .' I said.

I was looking for my lost hat.

'I wanted to go to the Opéra,' I said, 'but I haven't any tickets yet.'

I was amazed at my own presence of mind, I had never been to the Opéra, naturally, but Sabeth with her knowledge of human nature didn't suspect for a moment, although I had no idea what was on at the Opéra, and she took the money for the tickets, quite willing to do me a favour.

'If you feel like it,' I said, 'take two, and we can meet at seven o'clock – here.'

'Two?'

'It's supposed to be marvellous.'

I had heard that from Mrs Williams.

'Mr Faber,' she said, 'I can't let you do that . . .'

I was late for the conference.

I really hadn't recognized Professor O. when he suddenly stood there in front of me. 'Where are you off to in such a hurry, Faber, where are you off to?' His face wasn't even pale, but utterly changed. All I knew was that I knew that face. I knew the laugh, but where had I heard it? He must have noticed. 'Don't you remember me?' His laugh had become ghastly. 'Yes, yes,' he laughed, 'I've been through the mill!' His face was no longer a face, but a skull with skin over it, and even muscles that formed an expression, an expression that reminded me of Professor O., but it was a skull, his laugh was much too large, it distorted his face, it was much too large in relation to the eyes, which were set far back. 'Herr Professor!' I said, and had to take care not to add: 'I know, they told me you were dead.' Instead: 'Well, well, how are you?' He had never been so cordial, I looked up to him, but he had never been so cordial as now, while I stood there holding the taxi door, 'Spring in Paris!' He laughed, and I couldn't make out why he kept on laughing, I knew him as professor at the Swiss College of Technology, not as a clown, but every time he opened his mouth it looked as though he was laughing. 'Yes, yes,' he laughed. 'I'm better again now.' Actually he wasn't laughing at all, any more than a skull is laughing, it just looked like it, and I apologized for not having recognized him in my hurry. He had a tummy, a balloon of a tummy that welled out from under his ribs, all the rest was emaciated and his skin was like leather or clay, his eyes lively but sunken. I told him some sort of story. His ears protruded. 'Where are you off to in such a hurry?' he laughed and asked me if I wouldn't come for an *apéro*. His cordiality, as I have said, was also much too large; he was my professor back in the old days at Zurich, I looked up to him, but I really had no time for an *apéro*. 'My dear Professor . . .' I never used to call him that. 'My dear Professor,' I said because he was holding me by the arm, and I knew what everyone knew, but he didn't know apparently. 'Then some other time,' he said, and I knew for sure that this man was really already dead. I said, 'Yes, I should like that,' and got into my taxi.

The conference was of no interest to me.

I was always inclined to take Professor O. as a model; although not a Nobel Prize Winner, not one of the Zurich professors who was world-famous, he was nevertheless a true scientist. I shall never forget how we students stood around him in our white overalls and laughed at his pronouncement: 'A honeymoon' (he always said that) 'is quite enough, afterwards you will find everything of importance in publications, learn foreign languages, gentlemen, but travelling, gentlemen, is medieval, today we have means of communication, not to speak of tomorrow and the day after, means of communication that bring the world into our homes, to travel from one place to another is atavistic. You laugh gentlemen, but it's true, travel is atavistic, the day will come when there will be no more traffic at all and only newlyweds will travel about the world in a coach, no one else – you laugh, gentlemen, but you will live to see it!'

And there he suddenly was in Paris.

Perhaps that was why he kept laughing all the time. Perhaps it wasn't true that (as people said) he had cancer of the stomach, and he was laughing because for two years everyone had been saying the doctors had given him less than two months to live; he was sure we should meet again . . .

The conference lasted a bare two hours.

'Williams,' I said, 'I've changed my mind.'

'What's the matter?'

'Well, I've changed my mind . . .'

Williams drove me to the hotel, while I explained to him that I was thinking of taking a bit of a break after all, because of the springtime, a couple of weeks or so, a trip to Avignon and Pisa, Florence, Rome; he didn't behave oddly at all, on the contrary, Williams was as generous as ever; he immediately offered me his Citroën, because he was flying to New York next day.

'Have a nice time, Walter,' he said.

I shaved and changed. In case it was all right for the Opéra. I was far too early, although I walked all the way to the Champs Elysées. I sat down in a café next door, in a glazed verandah with infra-red heating, and had hardly been served my pernod when the stranger with the pony-tail walked past, without seeing me, likewise far too early, I could have called her . . .

She sat down in the café.

I was happy and drank my pernod without hurrying. I watched her through the glass of the verandah, she gave her order, then she waited, smoking, and once she looked at the clock. She was wearing her black duffle coat with the wooden toggles on cords and underneath it her blue evening frock, ready for the Opéra, a young lady trying out her lipstick. She was drinking a citron pressé. I was happier than I had ever been in Paris and I called the waiter so that I could pay and go – across to the girl who was waiting for me! And yet I was quite glad that the waiter was so slow in coming: I could never be happier than at the moment.

*

Since I have learned how it all came about, and particularly since becoming aware of the fact that the young girl who went with me to the Paris Opéra was the same child that we two (Hanna and I) didn't want to have on account of our personal situation, quite apart from the political state of the world, I have discussed with many and varied people their attitude to abortion, and I have discovered that, in the last analysis, they share my views. Nowadays abortion is a matter of course. In the last analysis, what would become of us without abortion? Advances in medicine and technology compel the most responsible people to adopt new measures. Mankind has trebled its numbers in a century. Previously hygiene was unknown. To conceive and bear and let the child die in the first year of its life, as nature decrees, was more primitive, but not more ethical. War against puerperal fever. Caesarean operations. Incubators for premature births. We take life more seriously than in earlier times. Johann Sebastian Bach brought thirteen children (or thereabouts) into the world, but less than fifty per cent of them lived. Men are not rabbits, it's the consequence of progress that we have to regulate things for ourselves. The world is threatened by overpopulation. My head physician was in North Africa, I quote his very words: 'If the Arabs ever stop relieving themselves round their dwellings, we must reckon with the Arab population doubling itself inside twenty years.' Nature everywhere ensures the survival of the species by overproduction. We have other

111

ways of ensuring the survival of the species. The sanctity of life! Natural overproduction (when we bear young haphazard, like the animals) becomes a disaster; not preservation of the species, but destruction of the species. How many people can the earth feed? An increase is possible, this is UNESCO's job, the industrialization of underdeveloped areas, but there is a limit to the possible increase. Let's take a look at the statistics. The reduction of tuberculosis, for example: through successful prophylaxis tuberculosis has been reduced from thirty per cent to eight per cent. God does the job with diseases, we have snatched the diseases out of his hand. The result: we must take procreation out of his hand as well. There is no cause for pangs of conscience, just the reverse: it is man's privilege and duty to act rationally and decide for himself. Otherwise we have to replace disease by war. An end to romanticism. Anyone who rejects abortion on principle is romantic and irresponsible. It should not be done thoughtlessly, that's obvious, but in the last analysis we must face facts, for example, the fact that man's existence is not least a question of raw materials. The fostering of an increased birth rate in Fascist states, but also in France, is a scandal. It's a question of living space. Automation mustn't be forgotten: we no longer need such a large number of people. It would be more sensible to raise living standards. Everything else leads to war and total destruction. Ignorance and unrealistic thinking are still very widespread. It is always the moralists who do the most harm. Abortion is the logical outcome of civilization, only the jungle gives birth and moulders away as nature decrees. Man plans. A great deal of unhappiness is caused by romanticism; think of the thousands of disastrous marriages still contracted out of sheer fear of abortion. What's the difference between contraception and abortion? Both are expression of the human will not to have children. How many children are really wanted? The fact that the woman would rather have it once it's there is a different matter, an automatic reaction of the instincts, she forgets she tried to avoid it and added to this is the feeling of power over the man, motherhood as an economic weapon in the hands of the woman. What does 'destiny' mean? It is ridiculous to attribute mechanico-physiological accidents to 'destiny', unworthy of modern man. Children are something we want or don't want. Injury to the woman? There is no physical injury, unless the abortion is carried out by a quack, if there is any psychological injury it is only because the person in question is dominated by moral or religious ideas. What we repudiate is the practice of idolizing nature. To be consistent, those who argue that abortion is 'unnatural' would have to say: no penicillin, no lightning-conductors, no spectacles, no D.D.T., no radar and so on. We live technologically, with man as the master of nature, man as the engineer, and let anyone who raises his voice against it stop using bridges not built by nature. To be consistent, they would have to reject any kind of operation; that would mean people dying every time they had appendicitis. What an outlook! No electric light bulbs, no engines, no atomic energy, no calculating machines, no anaesthetics – back to the jungle!

*

Of our trip through Italy I can only say that I was happy, because the girl, I believe, was happy too, in spite of the difference of our ages.

She scoffed at young men.

'Boys!' she said. 'You can't imagine what they're like – they think you're their mother, and that's frightful!'

We had stupendous weather.

The only thing that worried me was her hunger for art, her mania for looking at everything. No sooner were we in Italy than there wasn't a single place at which we didn't have to stop – Pisa, Florence, Siena, Perugia, Arezzo, Orvieto, Assisi. I'm not used to travelling like that. In Florence I rebelled and told her that frankly I thought her Fra Angelico rather mawkish. Then I corrected myself and said 'naïve'. She didn't deny it, on the contrary, she was delighted; it couldn't be naïve enough for her.

What I enjoyed was Campari!

I didn't even mind the beggars with mandolins.

What interested me was the way they built their roads and bridges, the new Fiat, the new station in Rome, the new Rapido rail motors, the new Olivettis . . .

Museums don't mean a thing to me.

I was sitting outside the Piazza San Marco, while Sabeth, out of pure spite I believe, went all over the monastery, drinking my Campari as usual. During the last few days, since Avignon, I had looked over all sorts of things, merely to be close to her. I saw no reason to be jealous, and yet I was jealous, I didn't know what a young girl like that might think. Was I her chauffeur? Well and good; in that case I was entitled to sit drinking Campari until my employer came out of the nearest church. I wouldn't have minded being her chauffeur, if it hadn't been for Avignon. I was often at a loss what to think of her. What an idea – to hitchhike to Rome! Even though she hadn't done it in the end, the very idea made me jealous. Would what happened in Avignon have occurred with any man?

I thought about marriage as never before . . .

The more I loved the child, the less I wanted to bring her to such a pass. I hoped from day to day that there would be a chance to talk to her, I was resolved to be perfectly frank, only I was afraid she wouldn't believe me or would laugh in my face. . . . She still found me cynical, I believe, even flippant (not towards her, but towards life in general) and ironical, which she couldn't bear, and there were times when I just didn't know what to say any more. Was she even listening to me? I really began to feel that the young were beyond me. I often appeared to myself a deceiver. Why? I didn't want to undermine her belief that Tivoli surpassed anything I had ever seen anywhere and that an afternoon in Tivoli, for example, was happiness squared; but I just couldn't feel that way about it. Her perpetual fear that I didn't take her seriously was the reverse of the truth, I didn't take myself seriously and something kept making me jealous, although I made an effort to be young. I asked myself whether young people today (1957) were totally different from those of our day, and I realized I knew nothing about the youth of today. I watched her. I followed her into museum after museum, simply to be near her, so that I could at least see Sabeth reflected in a glass case teeming with Etruscan potsherds, her young face, her earnestness, her joy. Sabeth didn't believe that I understood nothing about all that; on the one hand she had boundless trust in me, merely because I was thirty years older, a childish trust, and on the other hand no respect at all. I was vexed to find I expected respect. Sabeth listened when I told her about my experiences, but as one listens to an old man; without interrupting, politely, without believing, without getting excited. At most she interrupted in order to anticipate the story and so indicate that I had told her all that before. Then I felt ashamed. In general, only the future counted for her, and to a slight extent the present; but she had no interest at all in past experiences, like all young people. She didn't give a rap for the fact that there was nothing new under the sun, and for what had been, or could have been, learned from the past. I took careful note of Sabeth's hopes for the future and soon realized she didn't know herself what she hoped for, but merely looked forward to it. Could I expect from the future anything I didn't already know? For Sabeth it was all quite different. She looked forward to Tivoli, to seeing her mother, to breakfast, to the time when she would have children of her own, to her birthday, to a gramophone record, to definite things and especially to indefinite things; she took pleasure in everything that lay in the future. Perhaps this did make me envious, but it wasn't true that I took no pleasure in anything; I took pleasure in every moment that was in any real sense pleasurable. I didn't turn somersaults, I didn't sing, but there were certain things that I, too, enjoyed. And not only good food! I can't always put my thoughts into words. How many of the people I meet are interested in whether I'm enjoying myself, in my feelings at all? Sabeth considered that I went in for understatement, or that I hid my feelings. What I enjoyed most was her joy. I was often amazed at how little she needed to make her sing, really nothing-at all; she would draw the curtains, discover it wasn't raining, and sing. Unfortunately I once mentioned my stomach trouble; now she kept thinking my stomach was troubling me, with motherly concern, as though I was a child. Our journey wasn't easy, though often curious: I bored her with my experience of life, she made me old by waiting from morning to evening, wherever we were, for my enthusiasm . . .

In a large cloister (Museo Nazionale) I refused to listen to her Baedeker, I hoisted myself up on to the parapet and tried to read an Italian newspaper, I was fed up with this accumulation of stone debris. I went on strike, but Sabeth was still not convinced, she thought I was making fun of her when I confessed I knew nothing about art – she based her view on a saying of her Mamma's that anyone can respond to a work of art, except the cultured philistine.

'That's very kind of your Mamma!' I said.

An Italian couple strolling along the wide cloister interested me more than all the statues, especially the father, who was carrying their sleeping child on his arm . . .

There was no one else to be seen.

Birds twittered, otherwise it was as silent as the grave.

Then, when Sabeth had left me alone, I put away the paper, which I couldn't read anyhow, and placed myself in front of a statue to test her mother's statement. Anyone can respond to a work of art! But I found that her mother was wrong.

I was merely bored.

In the little cloister (glazed in) I was lucky. A whole group of German tourists, conducted by a Catholic priest, was crowding around a relief as though it was the scene of an accident, so that I grew inquisitive, and when Sabeth found me ('There you are, Walter, I thought you had gone off after your Campari already!') I told her what I had just heard the priest saying: *Birth of Venus*. The girl at the side, a flute-player, I found especially charming. . . . Charming wasn't the right word for a relief like this, thought Sabeth; she found it smashing, super, out of this world, shattering, terrific.

Fortunately some people came along . . .

I can't bear being told what I ought to feel; although I can see the subject under discussion, I feel like a blind man.

Head of a Sleeping Erinye.

This was my own discovery (in the same side hall on the left) without the help of any Bavarian priest; I didn't know the title, which didn't worry me in the least, on the contrary, the titles generally worry me, because I'm not familiar with classical names anyhow, they make me feel as though I'm doing an exam. . . . Here I found it – magnificent, impressive, superb, profoundly impressive. It was the stone head of a girl, so placed that when you leaned forward on your elbows you looked down upon it as though upon the face of a sleeping woman.

'I wonder what she's dreaming about . . . ?'

That was no way to look at art, perhaps, but it interested me more than the question whether it dated from the fourth or third century B.C. . . . When I went to look at the *Birth of Venus* again, she suddenly called out 'Stop!' I wasn't to move. 'What's wrong?' I asked. 'Stay where you are,' she said. 'When you stand there this Erinye looks much better, it's amazing what a difference it makes!' I must see for myself.

Sabeth insisted on our changing places. It really did make a difference, but this didn't surprise me: it was merely a matter of lighting. When Sabeth (or anyone else) stood by the *Birth of Venus* she cast a shadow, and because the light fell upon one side only, the face of the sleeping Erinye appeared far more wide awake, more lively, positively wild.

'Incredible what a difference it makes,' she said.

We changed places once or twice more, then I was in favour of moving on, there were still whole halls full of statues Sabeth wanted to have seen . . .

I was hungry.

It was no use talking about a *ristorante*, though it passed through my mind; I didn't even get an answer when I asked where Sabeth picked up all those clever words, my only answer was the words themselves – archaic, linear, Hellenistic, decorative, sacral, naturalistic, elemental, expressive, cubistic, allegorical, cultic, compositional and so forth, a whole highbrow vocabulary. Only at the exit, where there was nothing more to be seen but arches of ancient brick, simple but sound pieces of building construction that interested me, did she answer my question. Passing in front of me through the turnstile, she remarked casually, as always when she spoke of Mamma:

'From Mamma.'

Every time we went to a *ristorante* I found fresh pleasure in watching the girl, her delight with the salad, the childlike way in which she gobbled rolls, the curiosity with which she looked about her, chewing roll after roll and looking around, her solemn enthusiasm about an *hors d'oeuvre*, her high spirits . . .

As regards her Mamma:

We plucked our artichokes, dipped leaf after leaf in the mayonnaise and drew them between our teeth as I learned a few facts about the clever lady who was her Mamma. I wasn't very curious, to be frank, because I don't like intellectual ladies. I learned that she had actually studied philology, not archaeology, but she was working in an archaeological institute – she had to earn a living, because she was divorced from Herr Piper. I waited, my hand round the stem, to clink glasses; I wasn't in the least interested in Herr Piper, a man who lived in Eastern Germany out of conviction. I raised my glass and interrupted, 'Prosit!' and we drank ...

In addition I learned:

Mamma was also a Communist at one time, but in spite of this she couldn't get on with Herr Piper, hence the divorce, I could understand that, and now Mamma was working in Athens, because she didn't like the Western Germany of today either, I could understand that, and for her part Sabeth was in no way upset about the divorce, on the contrary, she had a hearty appetite as she told me about it and drank the white Orvieto – which I always found too sweet, but which was her favourite wine: *Orvieto Abbocato* ... She hadn't been particularly fond of her father, in fact Herr Piper wasn't her father at all, because Mamma had been married before and Sabeth was the child of her first marriage, her Mamma had been unlucky with men it seemed to me, perhaps because she is too intellectual I thought, but of course I didn't say anything; instead I ordered another half-bottle of *Orvieto Abbocato*, and then we talked about all sorts of things, about artichokes, Catholicism, *cassata*, the *Sleeping Erinye*, travel, the poverty of our time, and the best way to the Via Appia ...

Sabeth read from her Baedeker:

' "The *Via Appia*, the queen of roads built in 312 B.C. by the censor Appius Claudius Caecus, led via Terracina to Capua, from whence it was later extended as far as Brindisi ..." '

We had made a pilgrimage out to the Via Appia, two miles on foot, and were lying on one of these tombs, a mound of stones or debris covered in weeds, which fortunately wasn't

119

mentioned in Baedeker. We lay in the shadow of a pine tree smoking a cigarette.

'Walter, are you asleep?'

I was enjoying this relief from sightseeing.

'Look,' she said, 'that's Tivoli over there.'

Sabeth as usual was wearing her black jeans with the once white seams and her once white rope-soled shoes, although I had already bought her a pair of Italian shoes in Pisa.

'Does it really not interest you?'

'It really doesn't interest me,' I said, 'but I'll look at anything, my love. What isn't one willing to do on a honeymoon!'

Sabeth thought me cynical again.

I was quite content to lie on the grass, never mind about Tivoli, the important thing was to have her head on my shoulder.

'You're a restless creature,' I said, 'you can't stay quiet for even a quarter of an hour . . .'

She rose to her knees and looked round.

We heard voices.

'Shall I?' she asked, pursing her mouth as though to spit. 'Shall I?'

I pulled her down by her pony-tail, but she wouldn't put up with it. I also thought it a pity we were not alone, but there was nothing to be done about it. Not even if one was a man! She always had this funny idea: You're a man, aren't you? She evidently expected me to jump up and start throwing stones and drive the people away like a flock of goats. She was seriously disappointed, a child I was treating like a woman, or a woman I was treating like a child, I didn't know myself which it was.

'This is our place,' she said indignantly.

They were obviously Americans, I could hear their voices as the party wandered round our tomb; to judge by the voices, they might have been steno-typists from Cleveland.

'Oh, isn't it lovely?'

'Oh, is this the Campagna?'

'Oh, how lovely it is here!'

'Oh,' etc.

I sat up in order to peer across the undergrowth. The ladies' mauve-dyed hair interspersed with the bald patches of the gentlemen, who had taken off their panama hats – they must have broken out of an old age home, I thought, but I didn't say it.

'Our grave mound,' I said, 'seems to be a famous one.'

Sabeth indignantly:

'Look, there are more of them coming.'

She was standing, I was lying in the grass again.

'Look,' she said, 'a whole charabanc full!'

Sabeth was standing above and beside me. I could see her rope-soled shoes, then her bare calves, her thighs, which even when foreshortened were very slender, and her pelvis in the tight jeans; she was standing with both hands in her trouser pockets. I couldn't see her waist; because of the fore-shortening. But her breasts and shoulders were visible and above them her chin and lips and above these her lashes and the underside of the eye socket as pale as marble because of the reflected light from below, then her hair against the daz-zling blue of the sky, it looked as though her reddish hair would become entangled in the branches of the black pine tree. She stood like this, in the wind, while I lay on the earth. Slender and straight and speechless as a statue.

'Hello,' someone called out from below.

Sabeth answered gruffly: 'Hello.'

Sabeth couldn't believe her eyes.

'Would you believe it,' she exclaimed, 'they're having a picnic.'

Then, as though to spite the American besiegers, she dropped down and lay on my chest as if to sleep; but not for long. She sat up and asked whether she was heavy.

'No,' I said, 'you're light.'

'But?'

'No but,' I said.

'Yes,' she said. 'You're thinking something.'

I had no idea what I had been thinking; one is generally thinking something or other, but I really had no idea. I asked what she had been thinking. She asked for a cigarette, without replying.

'You smoke too much,' I said. 'When I was your age . . .'

Her likeness to Hanna struck me less and less frequently the more intimate we became, the girl and I. Since Avignon it had never occurred to me at all. At most I wondered how I could ever have thought she bore any likeness to Hanna at all. I studied her closely. Not the slightest likeness! I gave her a light, although I was convinced she smoked too much, a child of twenty . . .

She always answered mockingly:

'You talk like a heavy father!'

Perhaps I had (once again) been thinking that to Sabeth, when she lay on my chest and studied my face, I must appear an old man.

'Do you know,' she said, 'that was the Ludovisian Altar we liked so much this morning. It's madly famous!'

I let her give me a lecture.

We had taken off our shoes; I enjoyed the feel of our bare feet on the warm earth and everything else.

I thought about our Avignon (Hôtel Henri IV).

Sabeth with her open Baedeker knew from the outset that I was a technologist, that I was going to Italy for a rest. Nevertheless she read aloud:

' "The Via Appia, the queen of roads built in 312 B.C. by the censor Appius Claudius Caecus . . ." '

I can still hear her Baedeker voice.

' "The more interesting section of the road begins, the old paving is uncovered at several points, first comes the magnificent series of arches of the Aqua Marcia (cf. page 261)." '

She always turned back to the reference page.

At one point I asked:

'What is your Mamma's first name?'

She didn't allow herself to be interrupted.

' "A few minutes further on stands the tomb of _Caecilia Metella_, the most famous ruin of the Campagna, a circular structure sixty-six feet in diameter, resting on a square base and clad with travertine. The inscription on a marble tablet runs: Caecilia Q. Cretici f(iliae) Metellae Crassi, of the daughter of Metellus Cretius, step-daughter of the triumvir Crassus. The interior contained the burial chambers." '

She stopped and thought.

'I asked you a question,' I said.

'I beg your pardon.'

She shut her Baedeker with a bang.

'What did you ask me?'

I took hold of her Baedeker and opened it.

'Is that Tivoli over there?' I asked.

There must be an airfield on the Tivoli plain, even if it wasn't shown on the maps in this Baedeker; the whole time we heard engines, just the same vibrant hum as I used to hear above my roof garden on Central Park West, every now and then a DC-7 or a Super-Constellation flew over our pine tree, its undercarriage out ready to land, and disappear somewhere in the Campagna.

'The airfield must be over there,' I said.

I really wanted to know.

'What did you ask?' she repeated.

'What your Mamma's name is.'

'Piper,' she said. 'What else should it be?'

Of course I meant her first name.

'Hanna.'

She was already on her feet again, peering across the

undergrowth, both hands in her pockets and her reddish
pony-tail on her shoulder. She didn't notice the effect her
answer had on me.

'My goodness,' she exclaimed. 'You should see what
they're eating down there, there's no end to it – now they're
starting on the fruit!'

She stamped like a child.

'I say,' she exclaimed, 'I must go behind a tree for a
minute.'

Then I asked:

Did Mamma ever study in Zurich?

What?

When?

I went on asking questions, although the girl had to go
behind a tree for a minute. She answered rather unwillingly
but she left me in no doubt.

'Walter, I don't know that.'

Naturally, I was after precise dates.

'I wasn't there at the time,' she said.

She was amused because I wanted to know so much. She
had no idea what her answers meant to me. She was amused,
but that didn't alter the fact that Sabeth had to go behind a
tree for a minute. I sat there holding her forearm, so that she
shouldn't run away.

'Please,' she said, 'please.'

I asked my final question.

'Was her maiden name Landsberg?'

I had let go of her forearm. As though exhausted, I needed
all my strength just to go on sitting there. I was probably
smiling. I hoped she would run off.

Instead, she sat down and asked questions in her turn.

'Did you know Mamma, then?'

I nodded.

'No!' she said. 'Really?'

I simply couldn't speak.

'You knew each other while Mamma was at the university?' she asked.

She found it fantastic, simply fantastic.

'I'll write and tell her,' she said as she walked away. 'Mamma will be pleased . . .'

Today, now that I know everything, I find it incredible that I didn't know everything at that time, after our conversation by the Via Appia. I don't know what I thought during the ten minutes in which the girl was away. Of course I did some mental stocktaking. I only know that I felt like making for the airfield. Maybe I didn't think anything at all. It didn't come as a surprise, it merely brought certainty. I like to be certain of things. Once I'm certain of something I find it almost amusing. So Sabeth was Hanna's daughter! My first thought was that marriage was now out of the question. Yet I never thought for a moment that Sabeth might actually be my own child. It was within the bounds of possibility, naturally, but I never thought of it. More accurately, I didn't believe it. Of course I thought of it – our child at that time, the whole affair before I left Hanna, our decision that Hanna should go to a doctor, to Joachim. Of course I thought of it, but I simply couldn't believe it, because it was too incredible that this child, who shortly afterwards climbed up on to our grave mound again, should be my own daughter.

'Walter,' she asked, 'what's the matter?'

Sabeth was completely unsuspecting.

'You know,' she said, 'you smoke too much yourself.'

Then we talked about aqueducts.

Just to have something to talk about.

I explained about communicating pipes.

'Yes, yes,' she said, 'we had that too.'

She was highly amused when I demonstrated that if the ancient Romans had been in possession of this sketch on my cigarette packet, they could have done without at least ninety per cent of their brickwork.

We were lying in the grass again.

Aeroplanes flew overhead.

'You know,' she said, 'you really shouldn't fly back.'

It was our last day but one.

'We shall have to part some time, my dear child, in one way or another . . .'

I watched her.

'Of course,' she said. She sat up and pulled out a stalk of grass, then she stared straight in front of her; the thought that we must part didn't trouble her at all, it seemed, not at all. She didn't stick the stalk between her teeth, but wound it round her finger and said: 'Of course . . .'

There was no thought of marriage on her side!

'I wonder whether Mamma still remembers you.'

The idea amused her.

'You know, I can hardly imagine Mamma as a student,' she said. 'Mamma as a student living in a garret, you said, a garret – Mamma never told me about that.'

The idea amused her.

'What was she like in those days?'

I held her head so that she couldn't move, with both hands, the way you hold a dog's head. I felt her exert her strength, but it was no use, the strength of her neck muscles; my hands were like a vice. She closed her eyes. I didn't kiss her. I merely held her head. Like a vase, light and fragile, but growing heavier and heavier.

'Walter,' she said, 'you're hurting me.'

My hands held her head until she slowly opened her eyes to see what I was after – I didn't know myself.

'Seriously,' she said, 'you're hurting me.'

It was up to me to say something; she closed her eyes again – like a dog when you hold it fast like that.

Then I asked my question.

'Let me go!' she said.

I waited for her answer.

126

'No,' she said, 'you're not the first man in my life, you know that . . .'

I didn't know anything.

'No,' she said, 'don't worry . . .'

The way she pushed the flattened hair away from her temples, you might have thought her only worry was her hair. She took the comb out of her black jeans and combed it, while she stated casually: 'He's teaching at Yale.' She had a hair-slide between her teeth.

'And the other one,' she said with the hair-slide between her teeth, as she combed out her pony-tail, 'you've seen for yourself.'

She must have meant the ping-pong player.

'He wants to marry me,' she said, 'but that was a mistake on my part, you know, I don't like him at all.'

Then she needed the slide and took it out of her mouth, which now remained open but mute, while she finished combing her hair. Then she blew the comb clean, looked over towards Tivoli, and that was that.

'Shall we go?' she asked.

I really didn't want to remain sitting there, I wanted to straighten up, fetch my shoes, put my shoes on, my socks first of course, then the shoes, so that we could go . . .

'Do you think I'm bad?'

I didn't think anything.

'Walter!' she said.

I pulled myself together.

'That's okay,' I said, 'that's okay.'

Then we walked back to the Via Appia.

We were already sitting in the car, when Sabeth started off again ('Do you think I'm bad?') and wanted to know what was in my mind all the time. I inserted the ignition key to switch on the engine.

'Come,' I said, 'don't let's talk.'

Now I wanted to drive off.

Sabeth talked as we sat in the car without driving, about her Papa, about divorce, about war, about Mamma, about emigration, about Hitler, about Russia . . .

'We don't even know,' she said, 'whether Papa is still alive.'

I switched off the engine.

'Have you got the Baedeker?' she asked.

She studied the map.

'This is the Porta San Sebastiano,' she said. 'Now right, then we come to San Giovanni in Laterano.'

I switched the engine on again.

'I knew him,' I said.

'Papa?'

'Joachim,' I said, 'yes . . .'

Then I drove as ordered: to the Porta San Sebastiano, then right, until another basilica stood before us.

We went on sightseeing.

Perhaps I'm a coward. I didn't care to say any more about Joachim or ask any questions. In the silence of my mind I calculated ceaselessly (while I talked, more than usual, I think) until the sum worked out the way I wanted it: She could only be Joachim's child! How I worked it out, I don't know, I cooked the dates until the sum, as a sum, really worked out right. In the *pizzeria*, while Sabeth left me for a few minutes I gave myself the pleasure of checking the sum on paper. It was right; I had picked the dates (Hanna's announcement that she was expecting a baby, and my departure for Baghdad) in such a way that the sum was right; the only fixed date was Sabeth's birthday, the rest could be juggled till a weight was lifted from my heart. I know the girl found me jollier than ever that evening, positively sparkling. We stayed till midnight in this working folk's *pizzeria* between the Pantheon and the Piazza Colonna, where the singers came with their guitars after begging outside the tourists' restaurants and ate *pizza* and drank chianti by the glass; I bought them round after round and everyone was in high spirits.

'Walter,' she said, 'isn't this wonderful?'

On the way to our hotel (Via Veneto) we were jolly, not drunk, but distinctly gay until we reached the hotel, where they held the door open for us and handed over the room key in the alabaster hall, addressing us by the names we ourselves had given.

'Mr Faber and Miss Faber – good night!'

I don't know how long I stood in my room without drawing the curtains, a typical Grand Hotel room, far too big, far too high. I stood without undressing. Like a machine that receives the information 'Wash!' but doesn't function.

'Sabeth,' I asked, 'what's the matter?'

She was standing outside my door; without knocking.

'Tell me,' I said.

She was standing there with bare feet, wearing her yellow pyjamas, her black duffle coat thrown over them; she didn't want to come in, only to say good night again. I saw her tear-reddened eyes . . .

'Why shouldn't I love you still?' I asked. 'Because of Hardy or whatever his name is?'

Suddenly she burst out sobbing.

Later she fell asleep, I had covered her up, because the night outside the open window was cool; the warmth seemed to calm her, so that she really fell asleep, in spite of the noise in the street, in spite of her fear that I might go away. It must have been a street with traffic lights, hence the din – motor-cycles that revved up while they were stationary, then released the brakes, the worst thing was an Alfa Romeo that kept coming back and every time set off as though at the start of a race, making a noise that reverberated between the houses, it was barely quiet for three minutes at a time, every now and then the clock of some Roman church struck, then more hooting, the screech of brakes and tyres, revving up before starting off again, senseless, like the din made by urchins, then again the tinny roar, it really seemed as though the same Alfa Romeo was circling round us all night long. I became more and more wide awake. I lay beside her. I hadn't even taken off my dusty shoes and my tie, I couldn't move, because her head was resting on my shoulder. In the curtains shimmered the light of an arc lamp that swayed every now and then, and I lay as though being tortured, because I couldn't move; the sleeping girl had placed her hand on my chest, or rather on my tie, so that the tie dragged at my neck. I heard the hours strike one after the other, while Sabeth slept, a black bundle with hot hair and breath, and I was incapable of thinking ahead. Then came the Alfa Romeo again, hooting its way through the streets there was a screech of brakes, then it revved up, started and sent its tinny roar out into the night . . .

*

What did I do wrong? I met her on the ship as we waited for our table tickets, a girl with a dangling pony-tail who was standing in front of me. She caught my attention. I spoke to her, as people do speak to one another on a ship like that; I didn't run after the girl. I didn't delude her in any way, on the contrary, I spoke to her more openly than I normally do, about my bachelorhood for example. I made her an offer of marriage without being in love, and we knew at once it was stupid and we said good-bye. Why did I look for her in Paris? We went together to the Opéra and afterwards we had an ice, then, without keeping her any longer, I drove her to her cheap hotel in Saint-Germain, I offered to let her hitchhike with me, since I had William's Citroën, and at Avignon, where we spent our first night, we naturally stayed at the same hotel (anything else would have suggested an intention which I didn't have at all), but not even on the same floor; I never thought for a moment it would come to that. I remember exactly what happened. It was the night (May 13th) of the eclipse of the moon that took us by surprise; I hadn't read a newspaper, and we weren't ready for it. I said: 'What's wrong with the moon?' We were sitting outdoors and it was about ten o'clock, time to turn in, because we planned to leave early next morning. The mere fact that three heavenly bodies, the sun, the earth and the moon, occasionally lie in a straight line, which necessarily produces an eclipse of the moon, upset my equilibrium, as though I didn't know exactly what a lunar eclipse was. As soon as I saw the round shadow of the earth on the full moon I paid for our coffee, and we walked arm in arm up to the terrace above the Rhône, where we spent a whole hour, still arm in arm, standing in the night watching this perfectly intelligible phenomenon. I explained to the girl how it was that the moon, although totally covered by the earth's shadow, nevertheless emitted so much light that we could clearly see it, unlike the new moon, more clearly than usual in fact – not as the usual luminous disc, but definitely as a sphere, a ball, a body, an orb, an enormous mass in the empty cosmos, orange in colour. I can't remember all the things I said during that hour. But I do remember that the girl felt for the first time that I took us both seriously and kissed me as never before. And yet to look at it was rather oppressive, an enormous mass drifting, or hurtling, through space, which brought to mind the objectively quite correct idea that we on earth were also drifting, or hurtling, through the darkness. I spoke about death and life, I believe, in quite general terms, and we were both excited because we had never seen such a clear eclipse of the moon before, even I hadn't, and for the first time I had the bewildering impression that the girl, whom I had hitherto taken for a child, was in love with me. Anyhow it was the girl who that night, after

we stood outside until we were shivering, came into my
room ...

*

Then I met Hanna again.

(3 June in Athens.)

I recognized her before I was awake. She was talking to the
deaconess. I knew where I was and wanted to inquire
whether the operation had been carried out – but I was sleeping, completely exhausted, I was terribly thirsty, but I
couldn't say so. And yet I heard her voice speaking Greek.
They had brought me tea, but I couldn't take it; I slept, I
heard everything and knew that when I awoke I should face
Hanna.

Suddenly there was silence.

I was terrified the child might be dead.

Suddenly I was lying there with my eyes open. I saw the
white room, a laboratory, and the lady who stood by the
window, believing I was asleep and couldn't see her. Her
grey hair, her petite figure. She was waiting, both hands in
the pockets of her jacket, gazing out of the window. There
was no one else in the room. A stranger. I couldn't see her
face, only her neck, the back of her head and her short hair.
Every now and then she took out her handkerchief to blow
her nose and immediately put it away again, or crushed it in
her nervous hand. Apart from this she was motionless. She
wore glasses, black horn-rimmed glasses. She might have been
a lady doctor or barrister or something like that. She was
crying. Once she placed her hand under her horn-rimmed
spectacles as though to hold her face; for quite a time. Then
she needed both hands to unfold the wet handkerchief once
more, then she put it away again and waited, gazing out of
the window, where there was nothing to be seen but sunblinds. Her body was lithe, she would have looked positively
girlish if it hadn't been for her grey or white hair. Then she

took out her handkerchief again to polish her glasses, so that at last I saw her bare face, which was brown – apart from the blue eyes it might have been the face of an old South American Indian.

I pretended to be asleep.

Hanna with white hair.

Evidently, I really fell asleep again – for half a minute or half an hour, until my head slipped away from the wall so that I jumped – she saw I was awake. She didn't say a word, but just looked at me. She was sitting with crossed legs, her head in her hands, smoking.

'How is she?' I asked.

Hanna went on smoking.

'We must hope for the best,' she said. 'It's over – we must hope for the best.'

'She's alive?'

'Yes,' she said.

Not a word of greeting.

'Dr Eleutheropulos was here just now,' she said. 'He doesn't think it was an adder.'

She poured me a cup of tea.

'Come,' she said, 'drink your tea.'

Quite honestly, it never occurred to me that we hadn't spoken for twenty years; we talked about the operation that had been performed an hour ago, or we didn't talk at all. We waited together for a further report from the doctor.

I emptied cup after cup.

'You know they gave you an injection, too?' she said.

I hadn't noticed it.

'Only ten cubic centimetres, just as a prophylactic,' she said. 'Because of the oral mucosa.'

Hanna was altogether very matter-of-fact.

'How did it happen?' she asked. 'Were you at Corinth today?'

I was freezing.

'Where's your jacket?'

My jacket was lying beside the sea.

'How long have you been in Greece?'

I was astounded at Hanna; a man, a friend couldn't have asked in a more matter-of-fact tone. I tried to answer in the same tone. What was the use of assuring her a hundred times that I couldn't help it? Hanna didn't reproach me, she merely asked questions, gazing out of the window. She asked, without looking at me:

'How far did you go with the child?'

Yet she was very much on edge, as I could see.

'How do you mean, it wasn't an adder?' I asked.

'Come,' she said, 'drink your tea.'

'How long have you been wearing glasses?' I asked . . .

*

I didn't see the snake, I only heard Sabeth scream. When I got there, she was lying unconscious. I had seen Sabeth fall and had run to her. She was lying on the sand, knocked unconscious by her fall, I imagined, until I saw the bite above her breast, a small wound, three punctures close together. Then I realized what had happened. She was bleeding only slightly. Of course I immediately sucked out the wound, as prescribed, and I knew that a ligature should be applied between the wound and the heart. But how? The bite was above the left breast. I knew that the wound should be immediately excised or cauterized. I shouted for help, but I was already out of breath before I reached the road with the victim in my arms, after trudging through the sand; I was seized with despair when I saw the Ford drive past; I shouted as loud as I could; but the Ford drove past. I stood there out of breath with the victim in my arms, growing heavier every minute, I could scarcely hold her because she was a dead weight. It was the right road, but there wasn't a vehicle in sight. I got my breath back and went along this road of gravelled tar, first at a run, then slower and slower. I was barefooted. It was midday. I walked on in tears, until at last the cart came along. Up from the sea. Driven by a workman who spoke only Greek, but understood as soon as he saw the wound. I sat on the jolting cart, which was loaded with wet gravel, the girl in my arms just as she was, namely in a bikini and covered in sand. It shook the gravel, so that I had to go on holding the unconscious girl in my arms, and it also shook me. I asked the workman to hurry. The donkey was going no faster than walking pace. It was a rickety cart with crooked, wobbly wheels, a mile was an eternity; I sat facing the way we had come. But there was no sign of a car. I couldn't understand what the Greek was saying, nor why he stopped by a well; he tied the donkey up and signed to me to wait. I begged him to go on and not lose time; I didn't know what he had in mind when he left me alone in the gravel cart, alone with the victim, who needed serum. I sucked the wound out again. He had obviously gone to the huts to fetch help. I didn't know what help he imagined he could get, herbs or superstition or something. He whistled, then he walked on, because there was no reply from the huts. I waited a few minutes, then, without stopping to think, I ran on with the victim in my arms, until I was out of breath again and exhausted, I laid her down on the verge of the road, because there was just no sense in walking any farther; I couldn't carry her to Athens. Either a motor vehicle would come and pick us up, or it wouldn't come. When I sucked out the little wound on her breast again, I saw that Sabeth was slowly regaining consciousness: her eyes were wide open, but sightless, she only complained of thirst, her pulse was very slow, then she vomited with an outbreak of sweating. Now I could see the bluish-red swelling round her wound. I ran for water. All around there was nothing but gorse, thistles, olives on waterless land, not a single human being, only a few goats in the shade. I shouted and yelled in vain – it was midday, a deathly

silence; I kneeled down beside Sabeth; she wasn't unconscious, only very drowsy, as though paralysed. Fortunately I
caught sight of the lorry in time to run out into the road; it
pulled up – a lorry with a bundle of long iron pipes. Its desti-
nation was not Athens, but Megara, nevertheless it was
going in the right direction. I sat beside the driver, the victim
in my arms. The long pipes kept clattering and the pace was
murderous – less than twenty miles an hour on the straight! I
had left my jacket by the sea and my money in my jacket.
When he stopped in Megara I gave the driver, who also only
spoke Greek, my Omega watch to drive straight on without
unloading his pipes. We lost another quarter of an hour at
Eleusis, where he had to stop for petrol. I shall never forget
this run. I don't know whether he was afraid I should
demand my Omega watch back if I transferred to a faster
vehicle or what; but twice he prevented me from switching
over. Once it was a bus, a Pullman, once a limousine, which
pulled up when I signalled; my driver spoke to them in Greek,
and they drove on. He insisted on being the one to save us,
yet he was a wretched driver. On the hill leading to Daphni
he almost came to a standstill. Sabeth was asleep, and I didn't
know whether she would ever open her eyes again. At last we
reached the suburbs of Athens, but we were moving more
and more slowly; there were traffic lights and the usual traffic
jams, and our lorry with the long pipes projecting at the back
was less manoeuvrable than the rest, who didn't need serum;
it was a horrible town, a chaos of tramcars and donkey carts,
and of course our driver didn't know where to find a hospital,
he had to ask, and I began to think he would never get to it; I
closed my eyes or looked at Sabeth, who was breathing very
slowly. (All the hospitals were situated at the other end of
Athens.) Our driver, who came from the country, didn't even
know the names of the streets people told him, all I could
catch was 'Leofores, Leofores'; I tried to help, but I couldn't
even read. We should never have found it if it hadn't been for

the little lad who jumped on our running-board and showed us the way.

Then this antechamber.

A whole lot of questions in Greek.

Eventually the deaconess appeared, who understood English, a person of Satanic calm whose main concern was to know all our personal particulars.

*

The doctor who treated the girl reassured us. He understood English and replied in Greek; Hanna translated the important part for me: his explanation as to why it wasn't an adder (*Vipera berus*), but a snub-nosed viper (*Vipera aspis*), and his view that I had done the only possible thing in bringing her straight to hospital. As an expert, he didn't think much of popular remedies like sucking out the wound, excising or cauterizing it, or ligaturing the affected limb; the only reliable antidote was a serum injection within three to four hours with excision of the wound as a supplementary measure only.

He didn't know who I was.

I was in a sad state myself – sweaty and dusty like the workman on the gravel cart, with tar on my feet, not to mention my shirt, barefooted and jacketless; the doctor was concerned about my feet, which he left to the deaconess; he spoke only to Hanna, until Hanna introduced me.

'Mr Faber is a friend of mine.'

I was relieved to hear that the mortality from snake bites (adders and vipers of all kinds) is only three to ten per cent, even in the case of cobra bites it does not exceed fifty per cent, which is out of all proportion to the superstitious fear of snakes that is still so widespread.

Hanna was also somewhat reassured.

She told me I could stay with her.

But I didn't want to leave the hospital without seeing the

girl, if only for a minute; Hanna behaved very strangely (the doctor gave his consent at once) – she wouldn't let me stay in the sick-room for a minute, as though I was going to steal her daughter from her.

'Come,' she said, 'she's asleep now.'

Perhaps it was fortunate the girl didn't recognize us; she was sleeping with her mouth open (a thing she didn't normally do) and was very pale, her ear looked like marble, she was breathing in slow motion, but regularly, as though contentedly, and at one moment, as I stood by her bedside, she turned her head in my direction. But she was asleep.

'Come,' said Hanna, 'leave her.'

I should have preferred to go to a hotel. Why didn't I say so? Perhaps Hanna would also have preferred it. We hadn't even shaken hands. In the taxi, when I realized this, I said:

'Greetings!'

She smiled, as always at my bad jokes, creasing her forehead between her eyebrows.

She was very like her daughter.

Of course, I said nothing.

'Where did you meet Elsbeth?' she asked. 'On the ship?'

Sabeth had written about an elderly gentleman who had proposed marriage to her on the ship just before it reached Le Havre.

'Is that right?' she asked.

Our conversation in the taxi consisted of unanswered questions.

Why did I call her Sabeth? A question in response to my question, Why Elsbeth? In between came her statement, That's the theatre of Dionysos. Why did I call her Sabeth? Because Elisabeth seemed to me an impossible name. In between, remarks about broken pillars. Why Elisabeth of all names? I should never call a child Elisabeth. In between, traffic lights and the usual hold-ups. Well, that was her name, her father had chosen it, there was nothing to be done about it now. In between, she talked to the driver, who was cursing a pedestrian, in Greek. I got the impression we were going round in a circle, and it made me feel on edge, although we were no longer in any hurry. Then she asked:

'Did you ever see Joachim again?'

I thought Athens a dreadful city, like something in the Balkans, I couldn't imagine where people lived here, like a small town, or even a village in parts, Levantine, hordes of people in the middle of the street, then again desolation, ruins, and in between attempts to imitate a metropolis, dreadful; we drew to a halt soon after her question.

'Here?' I asked.

'No,' she said. 'I'll be back in a moment.'

It was the Institute where Hanna worked, and I had to wait in the taxi, without a cigarette; I tried to read the names over the shops and so on and felt like an illiterate, completely lost.

Then back into town.

Frankly, when Hanna came out of the Institute I didn't recognize her; otherwise of course I should have opened the door of the taxi for her.

Then her flat.

'I'll lead the way,' she said.

Hanna led the way, a lady with short grey hair and horn-rimmed spectacles, a stranger, but the mother of Sabeth or Elsbeth (my mother-in-law, so to speak!), every now and then I felt surprised that we addressed one another by our first names right away.

'Come,' she said, 'make yourself at home.'

This meeting after twenty years was something I hadn't reckoned with, nor had Hanna, incidentally she was quite right: to be exact it was twenty-one years.

'Come,' she said, 'sit down.'

My feet were hurting.

Of course I knew that sooner or later she would repeat her

139

question ('How far did you go with the girl?'), and I could have sworn that nothing had happened at all – without lying, for I didn't believe it myself, now that I saw Hanna in front of me.

'Walter,' she said, 'why don't you sit down?'

I stood out of spite.

Hanna pulled up the sunblinds.

The main thing was that the child was out of danger – I kept telling myself this all the time, whether I was talking about something else or saying nothing, smoking Hanna's cigarettes; she cleared some books away from the armchair so that I could sit down.

'Walter,' she said, 'are you hungry?'

Hanna as a mother . . .

I didn't know what to think.

'You have a nice view from here,' I said. 'So that's the famous Acropolis?'

'No,' she said, 'that's Lykabettos.'

She always had this habit, almost a mania, of being absolutely accurate, even over minor details: No, that's Lykabettos!

I told her so.

'You haven't changed!'

'You don't think so?' she asked. 'Have you changed?'

Her flat. Like a scholar's (I evidently told her that too; later, in the course of a conversation about men, Hanna quoted my remark about a scholar's flat as proof that I, too, considered science a masculine monopoly, all intellectual activity in fact); all the walls were covered with books, there was a desk covered with fragments of pottery bearing labels, but apart from this I saw, at first glance, nothing antiquarian, on the contrary, the furniture was thoroughly modern, which surprised me where Hanna was concerned.

'Hanna,' I said, 'how progressive you've become!'

She merely smiled.

140

'I mean it seriously,' I said.

'Still?' she asked.

There were times when I didn't understand what she meant.

'Are you still progressive?' she asked, and I was glad that at least Hanna was smiling ... I could see that the usual pangs of conscience you feel when you don't marry a girl were superfluous, Hanna didn't need me. She lived without a car of her own, but nevertheless contentedly: without a television set either.

'This is a nice flat you've got,' I said.

I mentioned her husband.

'Piper,' she said.

She didn't need him either, it seemed, not even financially. She had been living for years by her own work (I still haven't a clear idea of what this consists of, to be frank), not in luxury, but tolerably. I could see that. Her clothes could have stood up even to Ivy's scrutiny, and apart from an archaic wall-clock with a cracked face, her flat, as I have said, was thoroughly modern.

'And how are things with you?' she inquired.

I was wearing someone else's jacket which they had lent me in the hospital; I felt uncomfortably conscious of it all the time because it didn't fit me; it was too wide, because I am thin, and at the same time too short with sleeves like a boy's jacket. I took it off as soon as Hanna went into the kitchen, but my shirt didn't look nice either, it was blood-stained.

'If you would like a bath,' said Hanna, 'before I cook a meal ...'

She was laying the table.

'Yes,' I said, 'I've been sweating.'

She was touching and at the same time matter-of-fact; she turned the geyser on and explained how to turn it off, and she brought me a clean towel and soap.

'How are your feet?' she asked.

As she talked she busied herself with this and that.

'What do you mean, go to a hotel?' she asked. 'Of course you can stay here.'

I felt very unshaven.

The bath filled very slowly and steamed, Hanna added cold water, as though I couldn't have done that myself. I was sitting on a stool, as inactive as a guest, my feet were hurting badly, Hanna opened the little window, in the steam I could only distinguish her movements, which hadn't changed, not in the least.

'I always thought you were furious with me,' I said, 'because of what happened.'

Hanna was merely surprised.

'Why should I be furious? Because we didn't marry?' she said. 'That would have been a disaster.'

She positively laughed at me.

'Seriously,' she said, 'did you think I was angry with you, Walter, for twenty-one years?'

My bath was full.

'Why a disaster?' I asked.

Apart from this, we never referred to the fact that we once nearly got married. Hanna was right, we had other things to worry about.

'Did you know,' I asked, 'that the mortality from snake bites was only three to ten per cent?'

I was astounded.

Hanna had no use for statistics, I soon realized that. She let me deliver a whole lecture – in the bathroom – about statistics, and at the end all she said was:

'Your bath is getting cold.'

I don't know how long I lay in that bath with my bandaged feet resting on the edge – thinking about statistics, thinking about Joachim, who had hanged himself, thinking about the future, thinking until I shivered, until I didn't

know what I was thinking, it was as though I couldn't make
up my mind to recognize my own thoughts. I saw the flasks
and pots, the tubes, all sorts of feminine knick-knacks, I could
no longer picture Hanna, neither the Hanna of the old days
nor the Hanna of today. I was shivering, but I didn't fancy
putting my bloodstained shirt on again – I didn't answer
when Hanna called me.

What was the matter with me?

I didn't know myself.

Did I want tea or coffee?

I was worn out by the events of the day, hence my indecision, which wasn't like me, and hence the fantastic notions
(the bath as a sarcophagus – Etruscan!), a positive delirium of
shivering indecision . . .

'Yes,' I said, 'I'm coming.'

I hadn't really intended to see Hanna again; as soon as we
reached Athens I meant to go straight to the airport . . .

My time was up.

How I was to return the Citroën Williams had lent me,
which was now waiting in Bari, was a mystery to me. I didn't
even know the name of his garage in Paris.

'Yes,' I called out, 'I'm coming.'

But I just lay where I was.

The Via Appia . . .

The mummies in the Vatican . . .

My body under the water . . .

I've no use for suicide, it doesn't alter the fact that one has
been in the world, and what I wished at that moment was
that I had never existed at all!

'Walter,' she asked, 'are you coming?'

I hadn't bolted the bathroom door, and Hanna (I thought)
could easily come in and kill me from behind with an axe; I
lay with my eyes closed, to avoid seeing my ageing body.

Hanna was making a phone call.

Why couldn't things go on without me?

Later, as the evening passed, I once more talked as though nothing had happened. Without pretence; nothing had happened really, the main thing was that Sabeth's life had been saved. Thanks to serum. I asked Hanna why she didn't believe in statistics, instead of in fate and so forth.

'You and your statistics!' she said. 'If I had a hundred daughters, and all of them had been bitten by a viper, there would be some sense in it. Then I should only lose three to ten daughters. Amazingly few! You're quite right.'

And she laughed.

'I've only got one child,' she said.

I didn't contradict, nevertheless we almost quarrelled, suddenly our nerves gave way. It began with a remark on my part.

'Hanna,' I said, 'you're behaving like a hen.'

It just slipped out.

'Forgive me,' I said, 'but it's true.'

Only later did I realize what had annoyed me. When I came out of the bathroom Hanna was on the telephone, she had rung the hospital while I was in the bath – she was talking to Elsbeth.

I heard everything, without wishing to.

Not a word about me.

She was talking as though there was only Hanna, the mother who had trembled for her child and was now happy that the girl was gradually feeling better and could actually talk, they were speaking German, until I came into the room, then Hanna switched over to Greek. I couldn't understand a word. Then she hung up.

'How is she?' I inquired.

Hanna was greatly relieved.

'Did you tell her I was here?' I asked.

Hanna took a cigarette.

'No,' she said.

Hanna was acting very strangely, and I simply didn't believe that the girl hadn't asked after me; at least I had a right, it seemed to me, to know everything that had been said.

'Come,' said Hanna, 'let's have something to eat.'

What infuriated me was her smile, as though I hadn't the right to know everything.

'Come,' said Hanna, 'sit down.'

But I didn't sit down.

'Why are you offended when I talk to my child?' she said. 'Why?'

She was really acting (as I suppose all women do, no matter how intellectual they are) like a hen taking her chick under her wing; hence my remark to this effect; one word led to another, Hanna was furious at my remark, more crudely a woman than I had ever seen her. Her everlasting argument:

'She's my child, not your child.'

Hence my question:

'Is it true that Joachim is her father?'

No answer to this.

'Leave me alone!' she said. 'What do you want of me? I haven't seen Elsbeth for half a year, suddenly there's this call from the hospital, I go there and find her unconscious – and I don't know what has happened.'

I took it all back.

'You,' she said, 'what reason have you to talk to my daughter? What do you want with her anyway? What have you been doing with her?'

I could see she was trembling.

Hanna was anything but an old woman, but naturally I saw her withered skin, her lacrimal sacs, the crow's feet on her temples, they didn't disturb me, but I saw them. Her age suited her very well, I thought, especially in her face, apart from the skin under her chin, which reminded me of the skin of lizards. I took it all back.

I could well understand that Hanna was attached to her child, that she had counted the days until the child came home, and that it isn't easy for a mother when her child first journeys out into the world.

'She's no longer a child,' she said, 'it was I who sent her on this trip, one day she will have to live her own life, I quite realize that one day she won't come back . . .'

I let Hanna talk.

'That's the way things are,' she said, 'we can't keep life in our arms, Walter, you can't either.'

'I know,' I said.

'Then why do you try?' she asked.

I couldn't always understand what Hanna meant.

'Life goes with the children,' she said.

I had inquired about her work.

'That's the way things are,' she said. 'We can't marry again through our children.'

No answer to my question.

'Walter,' she said, 'how old are you now?'

Then came her statement that she hadn't a hundred daughters, but only one (as I knew), and her daughter had only one life (as I also knew) like every human being; she, Hanna, also had only one life, a life that was ruined, and I too (did I realize that?) had only one life.

'Hanna,' I said, 'we know that.'

Our food got cold.

Hanna was smoking. Instead of eating.

'You're a man,' she said. 'I'm a woman – that makes a difference, Walter.'

'I should hope so!' I laughed.

'I shall never have any more children . . .'

She said this twice in the course of the evening.

'My work?' she said. 'You can see for yourself, patching up fragments. That is supposed to have been a vase. From Crete. I stick the past together.'

146

I didn't consider Hanna's life ruined at all. On the contrary. I didn't know her second husband, this Piper, whom she had met after emigrating; Hanna hardly ever mentioned him, although (and this still surprises me) she bore his name: Dr Hanna Piper. Yet Hanna has always done what she thought best, and for a woman that says a great deal, I think. She led her life according to her own wishes. She didn't actually tell me why things hadn't worked out with Joachim. She called him a good fellow. Not a trace of reproach; at most she thought us all queer, men as a whole. Perhaps Hanna expected too much, where men were concerned, though I think she loved men. If there were any reproaches, they were self-reproaches; if Hanna could or had to live again, she would love men quite differently. She found it natural that men (she said) were mentally restricted, and only regretted her own stupidity in thinking each of them (I don't know how many there had been) an exception. Yet Hanna, to my mind, is anything but stupid. But she thought herself so. She thought it stupid of a woman to want to be understood by a man; the man (said Hanna) wants the woman to be a mystery, so that he can be inspired and excited by his own incomprehension. The man hears only himself, according to Hanna, therefore the life of a woman who wants to be understood by a man must inevitably be ruined. According to Hanna. The man sees himself as master of the world and the woman only as his mirror. The master is not compelled to learn the language of the oppressed; the woman is compelled, though it does her no good, to learn the language of the master, she merely learns a language that always puts her in the wrong. Hanna regretted having become a Ph.D. As long as God is a man, not a couple, the life of a woman, according to Hanna, is bound to remain as it is now, namely wretched, with woman as the proletarian of Creation, however smartly dressed. I thought her odd, a woman of fifty, philosophizing like a teenager, a woman who looked as elegant as Hanna, positively attractive, and on top

of this a personage, that was obvious, a lady of her standing –
I couldn't help thinking, for example, of how they had
treated Hanna at the hospital, a foreigner who had only been
living in Athens for three years, and yet they treated her
like a professor, a Nobel Prize winner! I felt sorry for her.

'Walter, you're not eating anything.'

I took hold of her arm.

'You proletarian of creation!'

Hanna refused to smile, she waited for me to let go of her
arm.

'Where,' she asked, 'did you go in Rome?'

I gave her a report.

The way she looked at me . . .

You might have thought I was a ghost, the way Hanna
looked at me as I reported on Rome, a freak with a trunk and
claws, a monster that drank tea.

I shall never forget that look.

She didn't utter a word.

I started talking again, because silence was impossible,
about the mortality figures for snake bite and about statistics
in general.

It was as though Hanna was deaf.

I didn't dare look into her eyes – every time I thought for
as much as a second (I couldn't think of it for longer) that I
had embraced Sabeth, or that Hanna, who was sitting in
front of me, was her mother, the mother of my mistress, who
was herself my mistress.

I don't know what I talked about.

Her hand (I was, so to speak, talking only to her hand) was
remarkable: as small as a child's hand, older than the rest of
Hanna, tense and slack, ugly, really not a hand at all, but
something maimed, soft and bony and flabby, wax with
freckles, not really ugly, on the contrary, something sweet,
but something alien, something horrible, something sad,
something blind, I talked and talked, I fell silent. I tried to

picture Sabeth's hand, but without success, I could only see what was lying beside the ash-tray on the table, human flesh with veins under the skin, which looked like crumpled tissue-paper, so crinkled and at the same time glistening.

I was dead tired myself.

'She's really still a child,' said Hanna, ' – or do you think she has already been with a man?'

I looked into Hanna's eyes.

'I wish her that,' she said, 'I wish her that.'

Suddenly she cleared the table.

I helped.

Regarding statistics: Hanna wasn't interested, because she believed in fate, I could see that straight away, although Hanna never expressly said so. All women have a tendency to superstition, but Hanna is highly educated; for this reason I was surprised. She talked about myths as we talk about the theory of heat, as though she were speaking of a physical law confirmed by daily experience, and hence in a positively casual tone. Without astonishment. Oedipus and the sphinx, portrayed in childlike fashion on a broken vase, Athene, the Erinyes or Eumenides or whatever they're called, were to her mind facts; there was nothing to prevent her from dragging them into a serious conversation. Quite apart from my ignorance of mythology and *belles-lettres* in general, I didn't want to argue; we had sufficient practical worries.

By 5 June I had to be in Paris.

By 7 June in New York.

By 10 June (at the latest) in Venezuela.

Hanna worked in an Archaeological Institute, gods were part of her job, I had to keep reminding myself of this; no doubt we too, without being aware of it, have a *déformation professionelle*. I had to smile when Hanna talked like that.

'You and your gods!'

She dropped the subject at once.

'I wouldn't leave,' I said, 'if it weren't quite certain that the child is out of danger, believe me.'

Hanna understood perfectly, it seemed, she washed the dishes while I spoke briefly of my professional obligations, and I did the drying up – just like twenty years ago, I thought, or twenty-one as the case might be.

'Do you think so?'

'Don't you think so?' I said.

I don't know how Hanna managed to make it twenty-one years. But I accepted her figure, so that she shouldn't keep correcting me.

'This is a nice kitchen,' I said.

Suddenly she repeated her question:

'Did you ever see Joachim again?'

Some time, obviously, I had to tell her that Joachim was no longer alive, but not just this evening, I thought, not just on the first evening.

I talked about something or other.

Our suppers in the old days in her room!

'Do you remember Frau Oppikofer?'

'Why?' she asked.

'It just came back to me,' I said. 'The way she always used to knock on the door with her broomstick, if I was still in your room after ten o'clock.'

The dishes were washed and dried.

'Walter,' she asked. 'Would you like some coffee?'

Memories are funny things.

'Yes,' I said, 'after twenty years one can laugh about it . . .'

Hanna put water to boil.

'Walter,' she asked, 'will you have some coffee?'

She didn't want to hear any memories.

'Yes,' I said, 'please.'

I couldn't see why her life was ruined. On the contrary. I always think it's wonderful when someone lives pretty much the way he once took it into his head to live. I admired her. Frankly, I had never imagined that anyone could earn money by philology and history of art. Moreover, you couldn't even say Hanna was unwomanly. Having a job suited her. Even when she was married to Joachim, apparently, she always worked, translations and suchlike, and certainly after emigrating. In Paris, after her divorce from Joachim, she worked for a publisher. When the Germans arrived, she fled to England and supported her child out of her own earnings. Joachim was a doctor in Russia and therefore unable to send her any money. Hanna worked for the German Service of the B.B.C. She is still a British citizen. Herr Piper owes her his life, it seems to me; Hanna got him out of some camp by marrying him (if I've got the story right), without stopping to think, because of her old love for Communists. Herr Piper proved a disappointment, because he wasn't a Communist, but an opportunist. As Hanna put it, ready to follow the party line to the point of treachery and now quite willing to approve of concentration camps again. Hanna only laughed, 'Men!' He was willing to serve under any flag, as long as he could make his films. In June 1953 Hanna left him. He simply didn't notice that he was proclaiming today what he had recanted yesterday, or vice versa; what he had lost was a spontaneous relationship to reality. Hanna didn't like talking about him, yet she told me all the more the less it interested me. Hanna thought this Piper's attitude to life sad, but typical of certain men – stone-blind, according to Hanna, lacking any contact. He used to have a sense of humour; now he only laughed at the West. Hanna uttered no reproaches; really she was only laughing at herself, at her love for men.

'Why do you say your life is ruined?' I asked. 'That's just your imagination, Hanna.'

She thought me, too, stone-blind.

'I can only see what is there,' I said. 'Your flat, your scientific work, your daughter – you should thank God.'

'Why God?'

Hanna was just the same as ever. She knew perfectly well what I meant. The way she played on words! As though it was a question of words. No matter how seriously you meant something, she suddenly got caught up in some word or other.

'Walter, since when have you believed in God?'

'Come,' I said, 'make some coffee.'

Hanna knew perfectly well that I had no use for God, and when it came to the point it turned out that she hadn't meant it seriously at all.

'What makes you think I'm religious?' she asked. 'Do you imagine there's nothing else left for a woman at the change of life?'

I made the coffee.

I couldn't picture what it would be like when Sabeth came out of hospital. Sabeth and Hanna and I in one room, for example in this kitchen. Hanna noticing how I had to hold myself back to avoid kissing her child, or at least putting my arm round her shoulders, and Sabeth discovering that I really (like a deceiver who has taken off his wedding ring) belonged to Mamma, although I had my arm round her, Sabeth's, shoulders.

'As long as she doesn't become an air hostess,' I said. 'I tried to talk her out of that.'

'Why?'

'Because it's out of the question for her to become an air hostess,' I said, 'a girl like Sabeth, who isn't just any run-of-the-mill girl . . .'

Our coffee was made.

'Why shouldn't she become an air hostess?'

All the time I knew that Hanna, her mother, was by no means delighted by this half-baked idea; she was only being stubborn to show me it was none of my business.

'Walter, that's her affair.'

Another time:

'Walter, you're not her father!'

'I know,' I said.

From the beginning I had been afraid of the moment when we should sit down because there was nothing else to busy ourselves with – now it had come.

'Come,' she said, 'talk.'

It was easier than I had imagined, almost commonplace.

'Tell me,' she said, 'what happened.'

I was astounded by her calm.

'You can imagine the shock I got,' she said, 'when I came into the hospital and saw you sitting there asleep.'

Her voice was unchanged.

In a certain sense everything went on as though we hadn't been parted for twenty years, or more accurately, as though we had spent these twenty years together, in spite of being apart. What we didn't know about each other were superficialities, not worth discussing, our careers and that sort of thing. What was there for me to say? But Hanna was waiting.

'Do you take sugar?' she asked.

I talked about my job.

'How did you come to be travelling with Elsbeth?' she asked.

Hanna is a woman, but she is different from Ivy and the others I have known, not to be compared; also different from Sabeth, who resembles her in many ways. Hanna is more understanding; without reproach as she looked at me. I was astonished.

'Do you love her?' she asked.

I drank my coffee.

'How long have you known I was her mother?' she asked.

I drank my coffee.

'You don't know yet,' I said, 'that Joachim is dead . . .'

153

I didn't mean to say it.

'Dead?' she asked. 'When?'

I had let myself be carried away, now it was too late, I had to tell – on this first evening, of all times! – the whole story of what happened in Guatemala; Hanna wanted to hear everything I knew, about his return from Russia, his work on the plantation, she had heard nothing from Joachim since their divorce; in the end I didn't tell her that Joachim had hanged himself, but lied and said *angina pectoris*. I was astonished to see how calmly she took it.

'Have you told the girl?' she asked.

Then there was an endless silence.

She had thrust her hand under her horn-rimmed spectacles again, as though to hold her face together; I felt like a beast.

'What fault is it of yours,' she said.

The fact that Hanna didn't even cry made everything worse. She stood up.

'Yes,' she said, 'we must get some sleep.'

It was midnight or thereabouts, I hadn't got my watch with me, but apart from that it was really as though time was standing still.

'I've put you in Elsbeth's room.'

We were standing in her room.

'Hanna,' I said, 'tell me the truth: is he her father?'

'Yes,' she said, 'yes.'

At the moment I felt relieved, I had no reason to suppose that Hanna was lying and for the moment (the future was in any case inconceivable) the most important thing was that the girl had received a serum injection and was out of danger.

I gave her my hand.

We were standing there utterly exhausted, Hanna too, I think, we had really said good night already – when Hanna asked again:

'Walter, how far did you go with Elsbeth?'

She knew perfectly well.

'Come,' she said, 'tell me.'

I don't know what I replied.

'Yes or no!' she demanded.

What was said was said . . .

Hanna was still smiling, as though she hadn't heard, I felt relieved that it was said at last, positively gay, or at least relieved.

'Are you angry with me?' I asked.

I would rather have slept on the floor, Hanna insisted that I should get a proper rest, the bed was made up with fresh sheets – all for the daughter who had been abroad for half a year: a new pair of pyjamas, which Hanna removed, flowers on the bedside table, and chocolate, which she left.

'Are you angry with me?' I asked.

'Have you got everything you need?' she asked. 'The soap is here . . .'

'I couldn't have known,' I said.

'Walter,' she said, 'we must get some sleep.'

She wasn't angry, it seemed to me, she even gave me her hand again. She was on edge, nothing more. She was in a hurry. I heard her go into the kitchen, where everything had already been done.

'Can I help at all?'

'No,' she said. 'Now you must sleep.'

Sabeth's room was rather small, but charming, with a lot of books and a view of the Lykabettos; I stood for a long time by the open window.

I had no pyjamas.

I'm not in the habit of nosing about in other people's rooms, but the photo was standing right on the bookcase, and after all I had known Joachim, her father, myself – so I took it down.

Taken in Zurich in 1936.

I had really made up my mind to go to bed, not to think any more, but I had no pyjamas, as I have mentioned, only my filthy shirt.

At last Hanna went into her room.

It must have been about two o'clock, I sat on the clean bed the way they sit on benches in public places, when they sleep, the down-and-outs, bent forward (as I always think when I see people sleeping in this way) like a foetus – but I wasn't asleep.

I washed.

Once I tapped on her wall.

Hanna pretended to be asleep.

Hanna didn't want to talk to me, at one point during the evening she told me to stop talking: 'Everything becomes so small, when you talk about it!'

Perhaps Hanna was really asleep.

Her letters from America – I mean Sabeth's letters – lay on the table, a whole bundle, New Haven postmarks, one from Le Havre, then picture postcards from Italy, I only read one, because it had fallen on the floor: greetings from Assisi (with no mention of myself) with a thousand kisses for Mamma, with a hearty embrace . . .

I smoked another cigarette.

Then I tried to wash my shirt.

I don't know what made me think it was all over, the worst anyhow, and how I could have imagined Hanna was asleep.

I washed as quietly as I could.

I admit that for quarters of an hour at a time I simply forgot what was going on, or at least it all seemed to me like a mere dream – when you dream you have been condemned to death and know it can't be true, that you have only to wake up . . .

I hung my wet shirt out of the window.

I looked at Joachim's face, a masculine face, pleasant, but I couldn't really see any likeness to Sabeth.

'Hanna,' I called, 'are you asleep?'

No answer.

I was shivering, because I had no shirt, it never occurred to me to take her dressing gown, which hung on the door, I could see it.

I saw all her girl's things.

Her flute on the bookshelf . . .

I put out the light.

Hanna had probably been sobbing for quite a while, her face pressed to the pillow, until she could stand it no longer. I jumped with fright when I heard her. My first thought: She was lying and I *am* the father. She sobbed louder and louder, until I went to the door and knocked.

'Hanna,' I said, 'it's me.'

She bolted the door.

I stood listening to her sobs and begged her in vain to come out into the hall and tell me what was the matter, but her only answer was sobbing, at first quietly, then louder again, there was no end to it, and when she did stop for a moment it was worse still, I put my ear to the door, not knowing what to think, at times she simply lost her voice, there was just a whimpering, so that I was relieved when she began to sob again.

I hadn't a pocket-knife or anything . . .

'Hanna,' I said, 'open the door!'

When I managed to force the door open with the poker, Hanna threw herself against it. She positively screamed when she saw me. I stood there stripped to the waist; perhaps that was why she screamed. Of course I felt sorry for her and I stopped pushing the door open.

'Hanna,' I said, 'it's me!'

She wanted to be alone.

Twenty-four hours ago (it seemed to me like a memory from my youth!) Sabeth and I were still sitting at Acro-Corinthus waiting for the sunrise. I shall never forget it. We had come from Patras and got out at Corinth to see the seven pillars of a temple, then we had supper at a nearby guest house. Apart from this, Corinth is little more than a hamlet. By the time we discovered there were no rooms free it was already getting dark; Sabeth thought it a wonderful idea of mine just to wander on into the night and sleep under a fig tree. Actually I had only meant it as a joke, but since Sabeth thought it a wonderful idea we really set off across country in search of a fig tree. Then we heard the barking of sheep dogs, uproar all around us, the flocks in the night; there must have been quite a number of the beasts, to judge by their yapping, and in the heights to which they drove us there were no fig trees, but only thistles and wind. Sleep was out of the question. I never thought night in Greece would be so cold, a night in June, downright wet. And on top of that we had no idea where it would take us, a bridle path leading upwards between rocks, stony, dusty, and hence as white as gypsum in the moonlight. Sabeth thought it like snow. We both agreed it was like yogurt! And above us the black rocks. Like coal, I thought. But again Sabeth compared them to something else; and so we chatted as we followed the path that led higher and higher. We heard the whinny of a donkey in the night. Like someone learning to play the 'cello, thought Sabeth. It reminded me of unoiled brakes. Apart from this there was a deathly hush; the dogs had fallen silent at last, now that they could no longer hear our footsteps. We saw the white huts of Corinth – as though somebody had emptied a bowl of lump sugar. I thought of something else, just to go on with the game. Then we came to a black cypress. Like an exclamation mark, thought Sabeth. I contradicted: exclamation marks have the pointed end at the bottom, not at the top. We roamed all night long. Without meeting a single human being. Once we were frightened by the tinkling of a goat, then silence returned to the slopes that smelt of peppermint, a silence accompanied by beating hearts and thirst, nothing but wind in the dry grass – like tearing silk, thought Sabeth. I had to think hard, and very often nothing occurred to me, than it was a point for Sabeth, according to the rules of the game. Sabeth almost always thought of something. The towers and crenellations of a medieval bastion – like the scenery at the Opéra! We passed through doorway after doorway, nowhere any sound of water, we heard our footsteps echoing against the Turkish walls, otherwise silence the moment we stood still. Our shadows cast by the moon – like paper cutouts, thought Sabeth. We always played to twenty-one points, as in ping-pong, then we began a new game, until suddenly, while it was still the middle of the night, we were standing on the mountain top. Our comet was no longer visible. In the distance lay the sea – like a sheet of aluminium, I said; Sabeth said it was cold, but nevertheless a wonderful idea not to spend the night in a hotel for a change. It was her first night out of doors. As we waited for the sunrise, Sabeth trembled in my arms. It is coldest just before sunrise. Then we smoked our last cigarette together; we didn't say a word about the coming day, which for Sabeth meant the return home. The first light of dawn appeared around five o'clock – like porcelain. It grew brighter every minute, the sea and the sky, not the earth; we could see where Athens must lie, the black islands in the light bays, water and land were parted, a few small morning clouds hung overhead – like tassels sprinkled with pink powder, thought Sabeth; I couldn't think of anything and lost another point. Nineteen to nine in Sabeth's favour! The air at this time of the morning – like autumn crocuses. I thought, like cellophane with nothing

159

behind it. Then we found we could make out the surf on the seashore. Like beer froth. Sabeth thought, like a ruche! I took back my beer froth and said, like fibreglass. But Sabeth didn't know what fibreglass was. Then came the first rays of the sun over the sea: like a sheaf, like spears, like cracks in a glass, like a monstrance, like photos of electron bombardment. But there was only one point for each round; it was no use producing half a dozen similes. Soon after this the sun rose, dazzling. Like metal spurting out of a furnace, I thought: Sabeth said nothing and lost a point. ... I shall never forget how she sat on that rock, her eyes closed, silent, letting the sun shine down on her. She was happy, she said, and I shall never forget the way the sea grew visibly darker, the Gulf of Corinth, and the other sea, the Gulf of Aigina, the red colour of the ploughed fields, the olives, like verdigris, their long morning shadows on the red earth, the first warmth and Sabeth, who embraced me, as though I had given her all this, the sea and the sun and everything, and I shall never forget how Sabeth sang!

*

I saw the breakfast Hanna had prepared and her note: Back soon, Hanna. I waited. I felt very unshaven and rummaged through the whole bathroom for a razor; there was nothing but flasks, boxes of powder, lipsticks, tubes, nail varnish, hairgrips; I caught sight of my shirt in the mirror – it looked more horrible than yesterday, the bloodstains were paler, but they had spread.

I waited at least an hour.

Hanna came back from the hospital.

'How is she?' I inquired.

Hanna was very strange.

'I thought I ought to let you go on sleeping,' she said.

Later, with no excuses:

'I wanted to be alone with Elsbeth, you mustn't be offended

by that, Walter, I've been alone with the child for twenty years.'

I didn't say a word.

'I'm not reproaching you,' she said, 'but you must understand that. I wanted to be alone with her. That's all. I wanted to talk to her.'

What did she talk about?

'A lot of confused stuff!'

'About me?' I asked.

'No,' she said, 'she talked about Yale, nothing but Yale, about a young man named Hardy, but it was all very confused.'

I didn't like what Hanna told me. The pulse had suddenly changed, yesterday it was rapid, today slow, far too slow, and added to this her face was flushed, Hanna said, her pupils very small and she had difficulty in breathing.

'I want to see her,' I said.

Hanna thought I ought first to buy a shirt.

I agreed to this.

Hanna made a phone call.

'It's all right,' she said. 'I'm getting the car from the Institute – so that we can drive to Corinth, you know, and pick up her things, yours too, your shoes and your jacket.'

Hanna behaved like a manager.

'It's all right,' she said. 'I've ordered a taxi.'

Hanna kept darting about, so that it was impossible to talk, she emptied the ashtrays, then she let down the sunblinds.

'Hanna,' I asked, 'why don't you look at me?'

She wasn't aware of it, perhaps, but it was so: that morning Hanna didn't look at me once. How could I help everything turning out like that? It was true Hanna didn't reproach or accuse me, she just emptied the ashtrays from the evening before.

I couldn't stand it any longer.

'Hanna,' I asked, 'can't we talk?'

I seized her by the shoulders.

'Hanna,' I said, 'look at me!'

Her figure – I started with surprise as I held her – was frailer, smaller than her daughter's, daintier, I don't know whether Hanna had grown smaller; her eyes were more beautiful, I wanted her to look at me.

'Walter,' she said, 'you're hurting me.'

I was talking nonsense, I could see from her face I was talking nonsense, and I was only talking because silence seemed to me even more impossible; I held her head between my hands. What did I want? I had no intention of kissing Hanna. Why did she struggle? I've no idea what I said. All I could see were her eyes, which were horrified, her grey and white hair, her forehead, her nose, everything dainty, noble (or whatever you like to call it) and womanly, nobler than in her daughter, the lizard's skin under her chin, the crow's feet on her temples, her eyes, which were not tired but merely horrified, and more beautiful than in the past.

'Walter,' she said, 'you're terrible.'

She said it twice.

I kissed her.

Hanna only stared at me, until I took my hands away, she said nothing and didn't even tidy her hair, she said nothing – she cursed me.

Then the taxi arrived.

We drove into the town to buy a fresh shirt, that is to say Hanna bought it, I had no money and waited in the car, to avoid having to show myself in my old shirt. Hanna was touching; she came back after a time to ask my size. Then we drove to the Institute, where Hanna, as arranged, picked up the Institute's car, an Opel, after which we set off for the sea to fetch Elsbeth's clothes and my wallet, or rather my jacket (chiefly for the sake of the passport), and my camera.

Hanna took the wheel.

In Daphni, that is to say a little way out of Athens, there was a grove where I could have changed my shirt, it seemed to me; Hanna shook her head and drove on. I opened the parcel.

What was there to talk about?

I talked about economic conditions in Greece, outside Eleusis I saw the great building site with a notice saying GREEK GOVERNMENT OIL REFINERY, all leased to German firms, which did not interest Hanna just then (or at any other time); but our silence was also unbearable. Only once she asked:

'Don't you know the name of the place?'

'No.'

'Theodohori?'

I didn't know, we had come by bus from Corinth and got out at a spot where the sea looked inviting, forty-one miles from Athens, I knew that; I remembered the milestones in an avenue of eucalyptus trees.

Hanna, at the wheel, relapsed into silence.

I was waiting for an opportunity to put on the clean shirt; I didn't want to do it in the car.

We drove through Eleusis.

We drove through Megara.

I talked about the watch I had given to the lorry-driver and about time in general; about clocks that were able to make time run backwards . . .

'Stop!' I said. 'This is it.'

Hanna stopped.

'Here?' she asked.

I only wanted to show her the slope where I had laid her down until the lorry with the iron pipes came along. A slope like any other, rock, covered in thistles interspersed with red poppies and beside it the dead straight road, along which I tried to run with her in my arms, black, gravelled tar, then the well with the olive tree, the stony field, the white huts with corrugated iron roofs.

It was midday again.

'Please,' I said, 'go more slowly.'

What had been an eternity walking barefoot took less than a couple of minutes in the Opel. Otherwise everything was the same as yesterday. Only the gravel cart with the donkey was no longer standing by the well. Hanna believed every word; I don't know why I wanted to show her everything. The point at which the cart emerged with its dripping gravel was easy enough to find, we could see the wheel ruts and the donkey's hoof marks.

I thought Hanna would wait in the car.

But Hanna climbed out and then walked along the hot, tarred road. Hanna followed me, I looked for the pine tree, then turned down through the gorse, I couldn't understand why Hanna wouldn't wait in the car.

'Walter,' she said, 'there's a trail!'

It seemed to me, however, that we hadn't come here to look for trails of blood, but to find my wallet, my jacket, my passport, my own shoes . . .

They all lay there untouched.

Hanna asked for a cigarette.

It was all the same as yesterday.

Only twenty-four hours later – the same sand, the same surf, gentle, just a succession of little waves running up the beach and scarcely breaking, the same sun, the same wind in the gorse – except that it wasn't Sabeth standing beside me, but Hanna, her mother.

'Did you go for a swim here?'

'Yes,' I said.

'It's lovely here,' she said.

It was dreadful.

*

As regards the accident I have nothing to conceal. It was a flat beach. You had to wade out at least thirty yards before you could swim, and at the moment when I heard her shriek I was at least fifty yards from the shore. I could see that Sabeth had jumped to her feet. I shouted: 'What's the matter?' She ran. After our sleepless night on Acro-Corinthus we had been sleeping in the sand, then I felt the desire to go into the water for a time in order to be alone while she slept. Before leaving I covered her shoulders with her underclothes, without waking her; for fear of sunburn. There was very little shadow here, an isolated pine tree; we made our bed in a hollow. Then, as was to be expected, the shadow, or rather the sun, moved, and I think that is what woke me up – I was in a sweat and all around lay the noonday silence, I woke with a start, perhaps I had had some sort of dream or imagined I heard footsteps. But we were utterly alone. Perhaps I had heard the gravel cart, the shovelling of gravel; but I couldn't see anything. Sabeth was asleep and there was no cause for alarm, it was ordinary midday, hardly any surf, just the low swish of waves seeping away into the shingle, occasionally the faint rolling of shingle, almost like the tinkling of a bell, apart from this there was silence broken by an occasional bee. I wondered whether it was sensible to go swimming when I had palpitations. For a time I stood irresolute; Sabeth noticed there was no one lying beside her and stretched, without waking up. I sprinkled sand over the back of her neck, but she was asleep. Finally I went for a swim – at the moment when Sabeth cried out I was at least fifty yards from the shore.

Sabeth ran without replying.

I didn't know whether she had heard me. Then I tried to run in the water! I shouted to her to stay where she was, feeling paralysed myself when I got out of the water at last; I stumbled after her until she stopped.

Sabeth was now on the top of the embankment.

She held her right hand on her left breast and waited without replying, until I climbed up the embankment (I had quite forgotten that I was naked) and came closer – then for some crazy reason, although I only wanted to help her, she slowly backed away from me, until (although I stopped at once) she fell backwards over the embankment.

That was the tragedy.

It was less than six feet, the height of a man, but by the time I reached her she was lying unconscious in the sand. She had probably struck the back of her head. It was only after several minutes that I noticed the bite, three tiny drops of blood, which I immediately wiped away; I at once put on my trousers, my shirt, no shoes, and then ran with the girl in my arms to the road, where the Ford shot past without hearing me.

*

Hanna stood at this scene of disaster smoking a cigarette, while I told her, as exactly as I could, what had happened, and showed her the embankment and everything; Hanna was amazing, like a friend, I had expected her, the mother, to curse me up hill and down dale although, looking at it objectively, I really wasn't to blame.

'Come,' she said, 'take your things.'

If we hadn't been convinced that the child was out of danger, of course, we shouldn't have talked like that on the beach.

'You know,' she said, 'that she is your child?'

I knew.

'Come,' she said, 'take your things.'

We stood there with the things on our arms; I was carrying my dusty shoes in my hand, Hanna our daughter's jeans.

I didn't know what I wanted to say.

'Come,' she said, 'let's go.'

I asked her:

'Why did you hide it from me?'

No answer.

Again the blue heat-haze over the sea – as yesterday at this time, midday with low waves that scarcely broke but only ran frothing up the beach, then the chink of shingle and the same thing over again.

Hanna understood very well what I meant.

'You forget,' she said, 'that I'm married.'

Another time:

'You forget that Elsbeth loves you.'

I found it impossible to take everything into account at the same time; but there must be *some* solution, I thought.

We stood there for a long time.

'Why shouldn't I find work in this country?' I said. 'Technologists are needed everywhere, as you have seen, Greece too is being industrialized.'

Hanna understood exactly what I was getting at, I wasn't thinking along romantic or moralistic lines, but in practical terms – of living under the same roof, pooling our resources and spending our old age together. Why not? Hanna had known at a time when I couldn't have had any idea, she had known twenty years ago; nevertheless she was more astonished than I.

'Hanna,' I asked, 'why are you laughing?'

There is always some sort of future, I thought, the world never comes to a stop, life goes on.

'Yes,' she said. 'But perhaps without us.'

I had taken her by the shoulders.

'Come,' she said. 'We're married, Walter, married. Don't touch me.'

Then we went back to the car.

Hanna was right, I always forgot something; but even when she reminded me, I was determined at all costs to get myself transferred to Athens or give notice, so that I could settle in Athens, even though at the moment I couldn't see myself how we could manage to live under the same roof; I'm in the habit of looking for solutions until they are found. . . . Hanna let me take the wheel, I've never driven an Opel Olympia and Hanna hadn't slept all night either; now she pretended to be asleep.

In Athens we bought some flowers.

Just before 3 p.m.

As we sat in the anteroom, where we were kept waiting, we still had no inkling whatever, Hanna unwrapped the paper from around the flowers.

Then we saw the deaconess's face!

Hanna stood at the window as yesterday, we didn't exchange a word, didn't even look at one another.

Then Dr Eleutheropulos came.

It was all in Greek; but I understood everything.

She died just before 2 p.m.

. . . Then Hanna and I stood beside her bed, we simply couldn't believe it, our child lay there with closed eyes, exactly as if she was asleep, but white as gypsum, her long body under the sheet, her hands by her hips, our flowers on her breast, I wasn't trying to comfort her, I really meant it when I said: 'She's asleep.' I still couldn't believe it. 'She's asleep,' I said – not speaking at all to Hanna, who suddenly screamed at me and struck out at me with her little fists, she was unrecognizable, I didn't defend myself, I didn't even notice her fists striking my forehead. What difference did that make? She screamed and hit me in the face until she could go on no longer, all the time I merely held my hand over my eyes.

*

As we know today, our daughter's death was not caused by the snake bite, which was successfully counteracted by the serum injection; her death was the result of an undiagnosed fracture of the base of the skull, *compressio cerebri*, resulting from her fall from the little embankment. There was injury to the *arteria meningica media*, a so-called epidural haematoma, which (I have been told) could easily have been put right by a surgical operation.

WRITTEN IN CARACAS, 21 JUNE TO 8 JULY

Second Stop

HOSPITAL, ATHENS
NOTES BEGUN ON 19 JULY

They have taken my Baby Hermes away and shut it up in the white cupboard, because it's the middle of the day, because it's the rest period. I'm supposed to write by hand. I hate handwriting. I'm sitting on my bed stripped to the waist, and my little electric fan (a present from Hanna) swishes from morning till night; otherwise there is deathly silence. Today it's 104 degrees in the shade again. These rest periods 1 P.M. to 5 P.M. are the worst. I have very little time left in which to bring my diary up to date. Hanna visits me daily, I jump with fright every time there is a knock on the white double door; Hanna, in black, comes into my white room. Why does she never sit down? She visits the grave every day, that is all I know about Hanna at the moment, and she goes to the Institute every day. The way she stands by the open window, while I have to lie down, gets on my nerves, and her silence. Can she forgive me? Can I make restitution? I don't even know what Hanna has been doing since it happened; she hasn't mentioned it once. I asked why Hanna didn't sit down. I don't understand Hanna at all, her smile when I ask her a question, the way she looks past me, at times I fear she is going mad. It was six weeks ago today.

8 June, New York.

The usual Saturday-night party at Williams's place out of town. I didn't want to go, but I had to; that's to say no one could really force me, but I went. I didn't know what to do with myself. Fortunately I had now heard that the turbines for Venezuela were at last ready for assembly and that I was to fly on as soon as possible – I wondered whether I was up to the job. While Williams, the optimist, had his hand on my shoulder, I nodded; but I wondered.

'Come on, Walter, have a drink!'

The usual business of standing around . . .

'A Roman holiday, oh, how marvellous!'

I didn't tell anyone my daughter had died, for no one knew this daughter had ever existed, and I wasn't wearing a black armband because I didn't want people to ask questions, because it didn't concern them.

'Come on, Walter, another drink!'

I was drinking too much.

'Walter is in trouble,' said Williams to those standing around. 'Walter can't find the key of his home!'

Williams thought I ought to act a part, better a comic part than none at all. You can't simply sit in a corner eating almonds.

'Fra Angelico, oh, I just love it!'

Everyone knew more than I did.

'How did you like the Masaccio fresco?'

I didn't know what to talk about.

'Semantics? You've never heard of semantics?'

I felt like an idiot.

I was staying at the Times Square Hotel. My name-plate was still on the apartment; but Freddy, the doorman, didn't know anything about a key. Ivy was supposed to have delivered it, I rang the bell at my own front door. I was in despair. Everything was open – offices and cinemas and the subway – everything except my home. Later I went out on a sightseeing boat, just to pass the time; the skyscrapers reminded me of tombstones (they always had), I listened to the loudspeaker – Rockefeller Center, Empire State, United

Nations and so on – as though I hadn't lived in Manhattan for eleven years. Then I went to the cinema. Later I travelled by subway, as usual. IRT, UPTOWN EXPRESS, without changing at Columbus Circle, although I could get closer to my flat with the INDEPENDENT, but I had never changed in eleven years, I changed where I had always changed, and on my way I dropped in at my Chinese laundry, where they still remembered me. 'Hello, Mr Faber.' Then back with three shirts that had been waiting for me for months to the hotel, where there was nothing for me to do, where I rang my own number several times – naturally without success! – then unfortunately I went to that party.

Nice to see you, etc.

Before that I went to my garage to ask whether my Studebaker was still there, but I didn't have to ask, I could see it from a distance (lipstick-red) in the yard between black fire-proof walls.

Then, as I have said, I went to the party.

'Walter, what's the matter with you?'

As a matter of fact, I've always hated these Saturday-night parties. I haven't the gift of being witty. But that doesn't mean I need a hand on my shoulder . . .

'Walter, don't be silly!'

I knew I wasn't up to my job. I was drunk, I knew that. They thought I hadn't noticed. I knew these people. Nobody would notice if you weren't there any more. I wasn't there any more. I was crossing Times Square (for the last time that night, I hoped) to ring my number again from a public call-box – to this day I can't understand how it was that someone answered.

'This is Walter,' I said.

'Who?'

'Walter Faber,' I said, 'this is Walter Faber.'

'Never heard the name.'

'Sorry,' I said.

Perhaps it was the wrong number; I took the enormous Manhattan directory, checked my number and tried again.

'Who's calling?'

'Walter,' I said, 'Walter Faber.'

The same voice answered as before, so that I said nothing for a moment or two; I didn't understand.

'Yes – what do you want?'

Nothing could really happen to me if I answered. I pulled myself together, before the other hung up, and asked, simply for something to say, what his number was.

'Yes – this is Trafalgar 4-5571.'

I was drunk.

'That's impossible!' I said.

Perhaps my flat had been let, perhaps the number had been changed, there were all sorts of possibilities, I could see that, but it didn't help me.

'Trafalgar 4-5571,' I said, 'That's me!'

I heard him put his hand over the mouthpiece and speak to someone (Ivy?), I heard laughter, then.

'Who are you?'

I asked back:

'Are you Walter Faber?'

In the end he hung up, I sat down in a bar, feeling dizzy, I couldn't take whisky any longer, later I asked the barman to look up Mr Faber's number and dial it for me, which he did; he handed me the receiver; I heard it ringing for a long time, then it was lifted.

'Trafalgar 4-5571. Hello?'

I rang off without uttering a sound.

My operation will rid me of all complaints for ever, according to statistics it is an operation that is successful in 96.4 out of 100 cases, and the only thing that makes me feel jittery is this waiting from one day to the next. I'm not used to being ill. Another thing that makes me jittery is the way Hanna comforts me, because she doesn't believe in statistics. I'm really full of confidence and at the same time glad I didn't have it done in New York or Düsseldorf or Zurich; I must see Hanna, or rather talk to her. I can't picture to myself what Hanna does outside this room. Does she eat? Does she sleep? She goes to the Institute every day (8-11 A.M. and 5-7 P.M.) and to our daughter's grave every day. What else does she do? I have asked Hanna to sit down. Why doesn't she speak? When Hanna sits down, not a minute passes before she needs something, an ashtray or a lighter, so that she gets up and stands again. If Hanna can't bear me, why does she come? She straightens my pillows. If it was cancer they would have got the knife to me at once, that's only logical. I explained that to Hanna and it convinced her, I hope. No injection today! I shall marry Hanna.

9 June. Flew to Caracas.

This time I flew via Miami and Merida, Yucatan, where there is a plane to Caracas almost every day. I broke my journey at Merida (with stomach trouble).

Then to Campeche again.

(Six and a half hours by bus from Merida.)

Back to the little railway station with the narrow-gauge track and cacti between the sleepers, where I waited for a train with Herbert Hencke two months ago.

I leaned my head against the wall with my eyes shut and my arms and legs stretched out; everything that had happened since the last time I waited for this train seemed to me like a hallucination – everything here was just the same.

The clammy air.

The smell of fish and pineapples.

The scrawny dogs.

The dead dogs nobody buried, the zopilotes on the roofs above the market place, the heat, the faint odour of the sea, the felty sun over the sea, over the land the bluish-white lightning flashing out of black clouds like the flickering light of a quartz lamp.

Once more the train journey.

Seeing Palenque again made me feel quite gay, everything was just the same: the verandah with our hammocks, our beer, our tavern with the parrot, they still remembered me, even the children recognized me. I bought and distributed Mexican sweets, once I even went out to the ruins, where in any case nothing ever changed, there was no one about, just the whirring birds as before, it was just the same as two months ago – the night too, after Palenque's diesel engine had fallen silent: the turkey in the enclosure outside the verandah, its squawking, because it didn't like the lightning, the deer, the black sow tied to a peg, the cotton-wool moon, the horse grazing in the darkness . . .

Over everything my idle thought:

If only it was that time, if only it was two months ago, two months during which nothing had changed here! Why can't it be April and everything else simply a hallucination on my part?

Then I drove alone in the Land Rover.

I talked to Herbert.

I talked to Marcel.

I bathed in the Rio Usumancinta, which had changed; it had more water and no bubbles on the surface, because it was flowing faster, and it was doubtful whether I could get the Land Rover across without being drowned.

I managed it.

Herbert had changed, I could see that at the first glance, he had a beard, but quite apart from that – his suspicious question:

'Man, what are you doing here?'

Herbert thought I had made the journey on behalf of his family, or the firm, to take him back to Düsseldorf; he couldn't believe I had simply come to see him, but it was true; I hadn't all that many friends.

He had broken his glasses.

'Why don't you mend them?' I asked.

I mended his glasses.

During the downpours we sat in the hut as though in a Noah's ark, without light, because the battery that in Joachim's day had also supplied the radio had long since run down, and news from the world didn't interest him in the least, not even news from Germany, the appeal of the Göttingen professors; I didn't discuss personal matters.

I inquired about his Nash.

Herbert had never been back to Palenque!

I had brought petrol, five cans for Herbert, so that he could drive away at any time; but he hadn't the slightest wish to.

He grinned into his beard.

We didn't understand one another at all.

He grinned when he saw me shaving with an old razor, because there was no electricity here and because I didn't want to grow a beard, because I had to move on.

For his part he had no plans.

His Nash 55 stood under the roof of dry leaves as before, even the ignition key was still inserted; obviously the Indians didn't even know how to start a car, nothing was damaged but it all looked like something out of a fairy story, so I got down to work at once.

'If you feel like it,' he said, 'then go ahead.'

Herbert went hunting iguanas.

I found the engine completely silted up by the heavy rains, everything had to be cleaned, everything was matted and slimy, there was a smell of pollen adhering to lubricating oil and putrefying, but I enjoyed the work.

The Maya children stood around.

They watched day after day as I took the engine to pieces and spread the pieces out on banana leaves on the ground.

There was lightning but no rain.

The mothers stared too, they never seemed to stop bearing, they stood there holding their last baby at their brown breasts, supported on their new pregnancy, gaping as I cleaned the engine, not saying a word, because I couldn't understand them.

Herbert came back with a bundle of iguanas.

They were alive, they were completely motionless until you touched them, their lizard's jaws tied together with straw, because they bite, when boiled they taste like chicken.

Evenings in the hammocks.

No beer, only this coconut milk.

Flashes of lightning.

My concern lest something should be stolen that was irreplaceable didn't affect Herbert; he was convinced they wouldn't touch any part of a machine. Not another word about an uprising! They're actually quite good workers, said Herbert, they do what they're told, although they are convinced it's quite useless.

He grinned into his beard.

The future of the German cigar!

I asked Herbert what he really proposed to do; did he intend to stay here or go back to Düsseldorf; what were his plans?

'Nada!'

Once I told him I had met Hanna, that I was going to marry Hanna; but I don't even know whether Herbert heard me.

Herbert was like an Indian.

The heat . . .

The glowworms . . .
We dripped as though in a Turkish bath.

The following day it rained, suddenly, only for a quarter of an hour, like the Flood, then the sun shone again; but the water stood in brown pools, and I had to push the Nash out of the hut so that I could work in the fresh air, I couldn't foresee that a pool would form at just this spot. Unlike Herbert, I couldn't see it as funny. The water came up above the axles, not to mention the parts of the engine I had taken to pieces and spread out on the ground. I was horrified when I saw it. Herbert gave me twenty Indians to mollify me and acted as though it was nothing to do with him, when I ordered trees to be cut down and the car jacked up so that I could get at it from underneath. I lost a whole day collecting the component parts, wading around in the murky puddle, feeling about in the warm mud; I had to do everything myself, since Herbert wasn't interested.

'Give it up!' was all he said. 'What's the use?'

I set the twenty Indians to work digging trenches to drain the water off; this was the only way of finding all the parts, and even so it was hard enough, since many of them had already sunk into the mud, or had been simply swallowed up.

His every other word was '*nada*'.

I let him talk nonsense, without answering. Without the Nash, Herbert was done for. I didn't allow myself to be infected and went on working.

'What would you do without a car?' I said.

When I had finally put the engine together so that it went, he grinned and said 'Bravo,' nothing else. He slapped me on the back and said I could have his Nash, he was making me a present of it.

'What use is it to me?' he said.

There was no stopping Herbert's fooling. He pretended to be a traffic policeman when I sat at the wheel of the jacked-up car to give everything a final test, while the Maya children stood all around, the mothers in their white shirts, all of them with nursing babies, and later the men too, standing in the undergrowth, all of them carrying curved knives, they hadn't heard an engine for months, I switched on and revved up, the wheels spun round in mid-air, Herbert signed to me to halt and I halted, I hooted and Herbert waved me on. The Indians (more and more of them all the time) stared at us without laughing as we fooled around, all of them quite mute, positively reverent, while we (for no good reason) played at rush-hour traffic in Düsseldorf.

Discussion with Hanna – about technology (according to Hanna) as the knack of so arranging the world that we don't have to experience it. The technologist's mania for putting the Creation to a use, because he can't tolerate it as a partner, can't do anything with it; technology as the knack of eliminating the world as resistance, for example, of diluting it by speed, so that we don't have to experience it. (I don't know what Hanna means by this.) The technologist's worldliness. (I don't know what Hanna means by this.) Hanna utters no reproaches, Hanna doesn't find the way I behaved towards Sabeth incomprehensible; in Hanna's opinion I experienced a kind of relationship I was unfamiliar with and therefore misinterpreted, persuading myself I was in love. It was no chance mistake, but a mistake that is part of me(?), like my profession, like the rest of my life. My mistake lay in the fact that we technologists try to live without death. Her own words: 'You don't treat life as form, but as a mere addition sum, hence you have no relationship to time, because you have no relationship to death.' Life is form in time. Hanna admits that she can't explain what she means. Life is not matter and cannot be mastered by technology. My mistake with Sabeth lay in repetition. I behaved as though age did not exist, and hence contrary to nature. We cannot do away with age by continuing to add up, by marrying our children.

20 June. Arrived in Caracas.

At last everything worked out: the turbines were on the spot together with the necessary labour force. I kept going as long as I could, and the fact that now, when the assembly took place at last, I had to drop out because of stomach trouble was bad luck but unavoidable; on the occasion of my previous visit (15 and 16 April) I was fit, but nothing else was ready. It was hardly my fault I couldn't supervise the assembly; I had to lie in bed at the hotel, which is no fun, for more than a fortnight. I had hoped to receive a letter from Hanna in Caracas. A telegram which I then sent to Athens also went unanswered. I wanted to write to Hanna and started several letters; but I had no idea where Hanna was staying and there was nothing left for me to do (I had to do something in that hotel!) but to draw up a report, without sending it off.

The assembly went off without a hitch – and without me.

Eventually the deaconess brought me a mirror – I got a shock. I've always been gaunt, but not emaciated as I was now; not like the old Indian at Palenque, who showed us the damp burial chambers. I really got a bit of a shock. Except while shaving, I rarely look in the mirror; I comb my hair without a mirror; nevertheless I know what I look like, or used to look like. My nose has always been too long, but I have never noticed my ears before. I'm wearing a pyjama jacket without a collar, that makes my back look too long and shows up the tendons of my throat when I turn my head, and the pits between the tendons, cavities I had never noticed before. My ears stick out like those of a shaven-headed convict. I can't seriously imagine that my skull has shrunk. I wonder whether my nose is pleasanter and come to the conclusion that noses are never pleasant, they're rather absurd, downright obscene. I can't possibly have looked like this in Paris (two months ago!), otherwise Sabeth would never have gone to the Opéra with me. And yet my skin is still quite bronzed, only the throat is rather whitish. With pores like a plucked chicken's neck. I still like my mouth, I don't know why, my mouth and my eyes, which, incidentally, are not brown, as I have always supposed, because it says so in my passport, but greyish-green; all the rest might belong to anyone who has been over-working. I have always cursed my teeth. As soon as I'm up and about again I must go to the dentist. Because of the tartar, perhaps also because of granuloma; I don't feel any pain, just a pulsation in my jaw. I have always worn my hair very short, because it's more practical, and it hadn't become any thinner at the sides, nor at the back. As a matter of fact I've had grey hair for a long time, silvery blond, that doesn't worry me in the least. When I lie on my back and hold the mirror above me I still look as I used to look; only a bit thinner, which is the result of the diet and not surprising. Perhaps it is the whitish light coming through the curtains that makes me look, as it were, pale under my tan; not white, but yellow. The only bad thing is my teeth. I have always been afraid of it; no matter what you do you can't stop them 'weathering'. It's the same with the whole of man – the construction is passable, but the material is no good: flesh is not a material, but a curse!

PS.
   There have never been so many deaths, it seems to me, as

184

*during this last quarter of a year. Now Professor O., whom I
spoke to personally in Zurich only a week ago, is also dead.*

PS.

*I have just shaved and then massaged my skin. It's rid-
iculous the ideas you get into your head from sheer idleness!
There's nothing to get upset about, I simply need fresh air
and exercise, that's all.*

9–13 July, in Cuba.

My reason for going to Havana: to change planes, because I
want at all costs to avoid flying via New York, KLM from
Caracas, Cubana to Lisbon, I stay four days.

Four days doing nothing but look.

EL PRADO.

The old street with the old plane trees, like the Ramblas in
Barcelona, the town out for its evening stroll, an avenue of
beautiful people, incredible, I walk and walk, I have nothing
else to do.

The yellow birds, their uproar at dusk.

Everyone wants to clean my shoes.

The Spanish Negress, who sticks her tongue out at me
because I am admiring her, her pink tongue in her brown
face, I laugh and say hello – she laughs too, showing her
white teeth in the red flower of her lips (if one may put it like
that) and her eyes, I don't want anything from her.

'How do you like Havana?'

My anger because they keeping taking me for an American, merely because I am white; the pimps walking along
in step with me:

'Something very beautiful! D'you know what I mean?
Something very young!'

Everyone strolling, everyone laughing.

Everything like a dream.

The white policemen smoking cigars; the sailors smoking cigars – lads with narrow hips in white trousers.

CASTELLO MORRO (founded by Philip II).

I have my shoes cleaned.

My resolve to live differently.

My joy.

I buy cigars; two boxes.

Sunset.

The naked boys in the sea, their skin, the sun on their wet skin, the heat, I sit and smoke a cigar, storm clouds over the white town, dark purple clouds, the last rays of sunshine lighting up the tall buildings.

EL PRADO

The green dusk, the ice-cream vendors; the girls sit (in groups) on the wall under the street-lamps laughing.

TAMALES.

This is maize wrapped in banana leaves, a snack which they sell in the street – you eat it as you walk along to save time.

My restlessness. Why do I feel restless?

There was nothing whatever for me to do in Havana.

My rest in the hotel – again and again – with showers, then unclothed on the bed, the draught from the electric fan, I lie smoking cigars. I don't lock my door; outside in the corridor a girl is singing as she does the cleaning, another Spanish Negress, I smoke incessantly.

My desire.

Why doesn't she come in?

My fatigue. I am too tired to fetch an ashtray, I lie on my back and smoke my cigar so that its whitish ash doesn't fall off, vertically.

PARTAGAS.

When I walk in the Prado again it is like a hallucination again – crowds of beautiful girls, the men very handsome too.

Splendid-looking people, a mixture of Negro and Spanish, I can't stop staring. Their erect and flowing walk, the girls in flared blue skirts, their white head-scarves, their Negresses' heels, their bare backs are precisely as dark as the shadows under the plane trees, consequently at first glance you see only their blue or lilac dresses, their white headscarves, their white teeth when they laugh and the whites of their eyes; their earrings flash.

THE CARIBBEAN BAR.

I am smoking again.

ROMEO Y JULIETA.

A young man, whom I first take for a pimp, insists on paying for my whisky, because he has become a father.

'For the first time!'

He embraces me, keeps repeating:

'Isn't it a wonderful thing?'

He introduces himself and wants to know my name and how many children I have, especially sons, I say:

'Five.'

He immediately insists on ordering five whiskies.

'Walter,' he says, 'you're my brother.'

We have hardly clinked glasses when he is off to buy the others a whisky, to ask them how many children they have, especially sons.

It's all like crazy.

At last the storm. As I sit alone under the arcades in a yellow rocking chair there is a rush of water on all sides, a sudden cloudburst with a gale, the avenue is suddenly empty of people, as though an alarm had sounded, the flapping of blinds, outside the rain spraying up from the pavement: a sudden bed of narcissi (especially under the street lamps), white.

Myself rocking and watching.

My delight at being here and now.

From time to time rain sprays in under the arcade, petal

confetti, then the scent of hot foliage and a sudden coolness on the skin, from time to time flashes of lightning, but the waterfall is louder than any thunder, I rock and laugh, wind, the rocking of the empty chair beside me, the Cuban flag . . .

I whistle.

My anger with America!

I rock and shiver.

THE AMERICAN WAY OF LIFE!

My resolve to live differently . . .

Flashes of lightning; afterwards it's as though you were blind. For a split second you see the sulphur-green palm trees in the gale, clouds, violet with the bluish glow of an oxy-acetylene torch, the sea, the flapping corrugated iron; the reverberation of this flapping corrugated iron, my childish delight in it, my sensual pleasure – I sing.

THE AMERICAN WAY OF LIFE.

Even what they eat and drink, these palefaces who don't know what wine is, these vitamin-eaters who drink cold tea and chew cotton-wool and don't know what bread is, this Coca-Cola people I can no longer abide . . .

And yet I am living on their money.

I have my shoes cleaned.

With their money.

The seven-year-old, who has polished my shoes once already, now like a drowned cat; I take hold of his fuzzy hair.

His grin . . .

His hair isn't black, more of an ashen grey, a brownish grey, young, it feels like horse hair, but frizzy and short, you can feel the childish skull underneath, warm, like stroking a shorn poodle.

He only grins and goes on polishing.

I love him.

His teeth . . .

188

His young skin . . .

His eyes remind me of Houston, Texas, of the Negro cleaning-woman who knelt beside me in the washroom after I had my attack of sweating and giddiness, the whites of her large eyes that are altogether different, beautiful like animals' eyes. The whole of her flesh.

We chat about different makes of car.

His nimble hands . . .

There is nobody else in sight but this boy and myself, all around us the Flood, he squats there shining my shoes with his rag so that it makes a slapping sound.

THE AMERICAN WAY OF LIFE.

Their ugliness in comparison with people like these here, their pink sausage skins, horrible, they only live because there is penicillin, that's all, the fuss they make as though they were happy because they're Americans, because they have no inhibitions, and yet they're only gawky and noisy – fellows like Dick, whom I have taken as a model! – the way they stand around, their left hands in their trouser pockets, their shoulders leaning against the wall, their glass in the other hand, easy-going, the protectors of mankind, their backslapping, their optimism until they are drunk and then hysterical weeping, sell-out of the white race, their vacuum between the loins.

My anger with myself!

(If only one could live over again.)

My night letter to Hanna . . .

The following day I drove out to the beach, it was cloudless and hot, midday with a gentle surf, the wash of the waves and the chink of the shingle, every beach reminded me of Theodohori.

I weep.

The water is clear, you can see the bottom, I swim with my face in the water so that I can see the bottom; my shadow on the bottom – a violet frog.

Letter to Dick.

What America has to offer: comfort, the best gadgets in the world, ready for use, the world as an Americanized vacuum wherever they go, everything is turned into a highway-with the world as a wall of posters on either side, their cities that aren't cities at all, lighting, next morning you see the empty scaffolding, humbug, infantile, an advertisement of optimism spread out like a neon carpet in front of the night and death ...

Later I hired a boat.

In order to be alone.

Even when they're in their bathing costumes you can see they've got dollars; their voices (as on the Via Appia) are unbearable, wherever you go you hear their rubber voices, the moneyed masses.

Letter to Marcel.

Marcel is right. Their fake health, their fake youthfulness, their women who don't admit to growing older, the way they use cosmetics even on corpses, their whole pornographic attitude to death, their President who has to laugh on every magazine cover like a pink baby, or else they won't elect him again, their obscene youthfulness ...

I rowed a long way out.

Heat haze over the sea.

Very much alone.

I read my letters to Dick and Marcel and tore them up, because they were not objective; the white scraps on the water; the white hairs on my chest ...

Very much alone.

Later, like a schoolboy, I draw a woman in the hot sand and lie down inside this woman, who is nothing but sand, and talk aloud to her.

'You wild girl!'

I didn't know what to do with this day, with myself, it was a queer day, I didn't recognize myself, I had no idea how

It had passed, an afternoon that looked absolutely like eternity, blue, unbearable, but beautiful, but endless – until I am once more sitting on the Prado wall (in the evening) with closed eyes; I try to imagine that I am in Havana, that I am sitting on the Prado wall. I can't imagine it, terror.

Everybody wants to clean my shoes.

Nothing but beautiful people, I gaze at them admiringly as at strange animals, their white teeth in the dusk, their brown shoulders and arms – their laughter, because they're glad to be alive, because it is a holiday evening, because they are beautiful.

My lust for looking.

My desire.

Vacuum between the loins.

I exist now only for shoeshine boys!

The pimps.

The ice-cream vendors.

Their vehicle: a combination of old pram and mobile canteen added to half a bicycle, a baldachin with rusty curtains; a carbide lamp; all around, the green twilight dotted with their flared skirts.

The lilac moon.

Then the business with the taxi. It was still early in the evening, but I couldn't bear to wander along any more like a corpse in the parade of the living, I wanted to get back to my hotel and take a sleeping powder; I beckoned a taxi, but when I pull the door open the two ladies are already inside, a black one and a blonde. I say 'Sorry!' and shut the door; but the driver jumps out and calls me back, 'Yes, sir!' he cries and pulls the door open again, 'For you, sir!' I have to laugh at so much service and climb in.

Our delicious supper.

Then the fiasco.

I knew it would happen sooner or later, afterwards I lie in my hotel – sleepless but relaxed, it is a hot night, from time to time I shower my body that is leaving me, but I don't take a sleeping powder, my body is still just good enough to enjoy the wind from the electric fan that sways this way and that, wind on my chest, wind on my legs, wind on my legs.

My haunting fear: cancer of the stomach.

Apart from this I am happy.

The din of birds at daybreak, I take out my Baby Hermes and at last type my UNESCO report on the erection of the turbines in Venezuela, which has been completed.

Then sleep till midday.

I eat oysters because I don't know what to do, my work is finished. I am smoking far too many cigars.

(Hence the pains in my stomach.)

The way I simply sit down on the Prado wall and get into conversation with a strange girl, in my opinion the same one who stuck her pink tongue out at me the day before yesterday. She doesn't remember. Her laughter when I tell her I'm not an American.

My Spanish too slow.

'Say it in English!'

Her long thin hands . . .

My Spanish is just enough for negotiations connected with my work. It's funny: I don't say what I want to say, but what the language wants. Her laughter at this. I am the victim of my limited vocabulary. Her astonishment, her positively kindly eyes when I myself feel astonished – at my own life, which seems, when put like that, so insignificant.

Juana is eighteen.

(Even younger than our child.)

Suiza – all the time she thinks it means Sweden.

Her brown arms stretched out backwards as a support, her head against the cast-iron street lamp, her white headscarf and black hair, her unbelievably beautiful feet; we are smoking; my two white hands interlaced over my right knee.

Her unaffectedness.

She has never left Cuba.

This is only my third evening here, but everything is already familiar – the green dusk with the neon signs, the ice-cream vendors, the checked bark of the plane trees, the birds with their twittering and the net of shadows on the ground, the red flowers of their mouths.

Her life's goal: New York!

The bird droppings from above.

Her unaffectedness.

Juana is a packer, a *fille de joie* only at week-ends, she has a child, she doesn't live in Havana itself.

Again the young sailors sauntering past.

I tell her about my daughter who has died, about the honeymoon with my daughter, about Corinth, about the viper that bit her over the left breast, about her funeral, about my future.

'I'm going to marry her.'

She misunderstands me.

'I thought she was dead.'

I explain.

'Oh,' she laughs, 'you're going to marry the girl's mother, I see.'

'As soon as possible.'

'Fine!' she says.

'My wife lives in Athens.'

Her earrings, her skin . . .

She is waiting here for her brother.

My question whether Juana believes in mortal sin, or in gods; her white laugh; my question whether Juana believes that snakes (speaking quite generally) are guided by gods, or by demons.

'What's your opinion, sir?'

Later the fellow with the striped Hollywood shirt, the youthful pimp, who has already accosted me, her brother. He shakes my hand: 'Hello, *camarada!*'

It doesn't mean anything, we are all good friends, Juana puts her cigarette under her heel and treads it out, her brown hand on my shoulder:

'He's going to marry his wife – he's a gentleman!'

Juana disappeared.

'Wait here,' he says and looks back over his shoulder to keep me where I am. 'Just a moment, sir, just a moment!'

My last night in Havana.

No time on earth in which to sleep!

I had no particular cause to feel happy, but I did. I knew that I am going to leave everything I am seeing, but that I shall not forget it: the arcade by night, where I rock and look, or listen as the case may be, a cab-horse whinnies, the Spanish house-front with the yellow curtains flapping out of black windows, then the corrugated iron again from somewhere, its reverberation going through my marrow, my pleasure at all this, my sensual delight, wind, nothing but wind shaking the palms, wind without clouds, I rock and sweat, the green palm tree is as pliant as a willow wand, the wind in its fronds makes a sound like knives being sharpened, dust, then the cast-iron street lamps that begin to whistle, I rock and laugh, their flickering and dying light, there must be a considerable draught, the whinnying horse can scarcely hold the cab, everything is trying to fly away, the sign on a barber's shop, brass, its tinkling in the darkness, and the invisible sea sending its spray over the wall, then every time thunder in its depths, over the top of this it hisses like an Espresso machine, my thirst, salt on my lips, a gale without rain, not a drop will fall, it can't because there are no clouds, nothing but stars, nothing but the hot, dry dust in the air, air like an oven, I rock to and fro and drink my Scotch, one only, I can't take any more, I rock and sing. For hours on end. I sing! I can't sing, but nobody hears me, the cab-horse on the empty tarmac, the last girls in their flying skirts, their brown legs when their skirts fly up, their black hair that also flies out behind them, and the green Venetian blind that has torn itself free, their white laughter in the dust and the way it skids over the surface of the street out towards the sea, the raspberry light in the dust above the white town in the night, the heat, the Cuban flag – I rock and sing, nothing else, the rocking of the empty chair beside me, the whistling cast iron, the eddy of petals. I sing the praises of life!

Saturday, 13 July. Flew on.

Morning in the Prado, after I have been to the bank to change money, the empty avenue, slippery with bird droppings and white petals . . .

The sun . . .

Everything at work.

The birds . . .

Then a man who asks me for a light for his cigar, he is in a hurry but nevertheless he walks along with me and asks me:

'How do you like Havana?'

'I love it,' I say.

Another pimp, his personal interest in me.

'You're happy, aren't you?'

He admires my camera.

'Something very beautiful! D'you know what I mean? Something very young!'

When I tell him I'm travelling on, he wants to know when I have to be at the airport.

'Ten o'clock, my friend, ten o'clock.'

A glance at his watch.

'Well,' he says, 'it's nine o'clock now, sir, that's plenty of time!'

I saunter down to the sea again.

Far out to sea the fishing-boats . . .

Parting.

I sit on one of the concrete breakwaters again and smoke another cigar – I'm not filming anything any more. What's the use! Hanna is right: afterwards you have to look at it as a film, when it's all no longer there, and everything passes away . . .

Parting.

Hanna has been here. I told her she looked like a bride. Hanna in white! She has suddenly stopped wearing mourning when she comes to see me; her excuse is that it is too hot outside. I've talked to her so much about zopilotes, now she doesn't want to sit by my bed like a black vulture – she thinks I don't notice her charming thoughtfulness, because in the past (a few weeks ago) I failed to notice so much. Hanna has told me a lot.

PS.

Once as a child, Hanna wrestled with her brother and swore never to love a man, because her younger brother succeeded in throwing Hanna on her back. She was furious with God for having made boys stronger than girls, she thought him unfair, not her brother, but God. Hanna made up her mind to be cleverer than all the boys of Munich-Schwabing and founded a secret girls' club to do away with Jehovah. Whatever happened, they were only prepared to consider a heaven in which there were also goddesses. Hanna turned first to the Mother of God, as the result of seeing religious pictures in which Mary reigned in the centre; she knelt down like her Catholic girl friends and crossed herself, which had to be kept secret from Papa. The only man she

trusted was an old man named Armin, who played a certain
part in Hanna's childhood. I didn't know Hanna had a
brother. Hanna tells me he lives in Canada and is very
capable, I believe he puts them all on their backs. I asked how
she lived with Joachim in those days, where and for how
long. I asked a great many questions; Hanna always
answered: 'But you know that!' She told me most about
Armin. He was a blind man. Hanna still loves him, although
he died, or disappeared, long ago. Hanna was still a schoolgirl
in long socks, she used to meet him regularly in the Englische
Garten, where he always sat on the same bench, and then
guided him through Munich. He loved Munich. He was old,
downright ancient by her standards at the time – between
fifty and sixty. They were always short of time, every Tuesday and Friday, when Hanna had her violin lessons, and they
met in all weathers, she guided him and showed him the shop
windows. Armin was totally blind, but he could picture
everything that was described to him. Hanna said: 'It was
simply wonderful to walk through the world with him.' I also
asked how the birth of our child went. I wasn't there: how
could I picture it? Of course Joachim was there. He knew he
wasn't the father; but he was like a real father. An easy birth,
according to Hanna; she remembered only that she was very
happy to be a mother. One thing I didn't know: my mother
knew the child was by me, no one else, in Zurich, my father
had no idea. I asked why my mother never mentioned in any
of her letters that she knew. A pact between women? They
simply don't mention things we shouldn't understand and
treat us like children. According to Hanna my parents were
in every way different from what I imagined; at any rate
towards Hanna. When Hanna talks about my mother I can
only listen. Like a blind man! They kept up a correspondence
for years, Hanna and my mother, who incidentally didn't die
of an embolism, as I thought. Hanna was surprised to find

how much I didn't know. Hanna went to her funeral in 1937. Her love of the ancient Greeks, says Hanna, also began in the Englische Garten; Armin knew Greek and the girl had to read to him out of her school books, so that he could learn it by heart. This was, so to speak, his way of raping her. He never took Hanna to his home. She doesn't know where he lived or how. Hanna used to meet him in the Englische Garten and left him in the Englische Garten, and no one in the world knew of their plan to go to Greece together, Armin and she, as soon as she was grown-up and free; Hanna was going to show him the Greek temples. Whether the old man was in earnest is uncertain; Hanna was in earnest. Hanna in long socks! At one time, I remember, there used to sit in the Café Odéon, Zurich, an old gentleman whom Hanna regularly had to fetch and take to the tram. As a matter of fact I used to hate this Café Odéon, it was full of emigrants and intellectuals – bohemians. Professors and the old tarts who catered for businessmen up from the country. I only went into this café to please Hanna. He lived in the Pension Fontana, I used to wait concealed in a little shelter in the Goriastrasse until Hanna had delivered her old uncle. So that was Armin! I never really noticed him. 'But he noticed you,' said Hanna. Hanna continues to talk of Armin as though he were still alive, as though he saw everything. I asked why Hanna never went with him to Greece. Hanna laughed in my face, as if it had all been a childish game. In Paris (1937 to 1940) Hanna lived with a French writer who is supposed to be quite well known; I've forgotten his name. What I didn't know was that Hanna went to Moscow (1948) with her second husband. She once passed through Zurich again (1953) without our daughter; she liked Zurich, as though nothing had ever happened there; she also visited the Café Odéon. I asked how Armin died. Hanna met him again in London (1942). Armin was planning to emigrate and Hanna actually took him aboard the ship, which he couldn't see and which was probably *sunk by a German U-boat; anyhow, it never reached port.*

15 July, Düsseldorf.

What the young technician whom the gentlemen of Hencke-Bosch placed at my disposal thought of me, I don't know; I can only say that I kept a grip of myself that morning as long as I could.

A multi-storey building with chromium fittings.

I considered it my duty as a friend to inform the gentlemen in Düsseldorf what their plantation in Guatemala looked like, that is to say I flew from Lisbon to Düsseldorf without thinking what I was really going to do or say in Düsseldorf, and now there I sat after a friendly reception.

'I've got some films,' I said.

I had the impression they had already written the plantation off; they were feigning interest purely out of politeness.

'How long will your films take?'

I was really only a nuisance.

'What do you mean accident?' I said. 'My friend hanged himself – didn't you know that?'

Of course they knew.

I had the feeling they didn't take me seriously, but there was no getting out of it now, my coloured films from Guatemala had to be shown. The technician who had been detailed to get everything ready in the board-room only irritated me; he was very young and a pleasant fellow, but superfluous, I needed a projector, a screen and a cable, I didn't need a technician.

'Thank you,' I said.

'Not at all, sir,' he said.

'I know the projector,' I said.

I couldn't get rid of him.

It was the first time I had seen the films myself (none of them cut yet), well aware that they were full of repetition, inevitably; I was amazed how many sunsets there were, three in the Tamaulipas desert alone, anyone would have thought I was travelling in sunsets, ridiculous; I felt downright ashamed of what the young technician must think of me, hence my impatience . . .

'It won't go any clearer, sir.'

Our Land Rover on the Rio Usumancinta.

Zopilotes at work.

'Go on,' I said, 'please.'

Then the first Indians who appeared that morning and told us their señor was dead, then the end of the reel – change of reel, which took some time; while we chatted about Ektachrome. I was sitting in an armchair smoking, because I had nothing to do, beside me the empty directors' chairs; only they didn't rock to and fro in the wind.

'Please,' I said. 'Carry on.'

Now Joachim dangling from the wire.

'Stop,' I said, 'please!'

The shot was unfortunately very dark, you couldn't see at once what it was, there was not enough light, because it was taken inside the hut with the same stop as had been used before for the zopilotes on the donkey outside in the morning sun. I said:

'That is Dr Joachim Hencke.'

He looked at the screen.

'It won't go any clearer, sir – I'm sorry.'

That was all he had to say.

'Go on, please,' I said.

Again Joachim at the end of the wire, but this time from the side, so that you could see better what was going on; it was curious, it not only made no impression on my young technician, it made none on me either, it was just a film such

200

as one had seen many times before, a newsreel, the stench was missing, it lacked reality, the young technician and I discussed lighting, meanwhile the grave appeared, surrounded by praying Indians, the whole thing much too long-winded, then suddenly the Palenque ruins, the Palenque parrot. End of the reel.

'Do you think we could have a window open,' I said. 'It's like the tropics in here.'

'Very good, sir.'

The trouble was that the customs had muddled up my reels and also that the more recent reels (taken after my sea voyage) had no labels on them; I only wanted to show the gentlemen of Hencke-Bosch, who were due at 11.30, the films dealing with Guatemala. What I was looking for now was my last visit to Herbert.

'Stop,' I said. 'That's Greece.'

'Greece?'

'Stop!' I shouted. 'Stop!'

'Very good, sir.'

The young man was getting on my nerves with his obliging 'Very good, sir,' his condescending 'Very good, sir,' as though he was the only man who understood a projector like this, the nonsense he talked about optics, which he knew nothing about, but especially his 'Very good, sir' and his air of superiority.

'There's nothing for it, sir, we must run them all through and look at them, if the reels aren't labelled.'

It wasn't his fault that the reels weren't labelled; I had to admit that.

'It begins with Herbert Hencke,' I said, 'with Herbert Hencke, a man with a beard in a hammock – as far as I remember.'

Lights out, darkness, the hum of the projector.

It was a game of pure chance! The first few feet were enough: Ivy on the pier in Manhattan, Ivy waving taken with my tele-lens, morning sun on the Hudson, the black tugs, Manhattan skyline, gulls . . .

'Stop,' I said. 'Next one, please.'

Change of reels.

'You must have been half-way around the world, sir, I'd like to do that . . .'

It was 11 o'clock.

I had to take my tablets, in order to be fit when the gentlemen of the firm arrived, tablets without water, I didn't want anyone to notice.

'No,' I said, 'not that one either.'

Another change of reels.

'That was the station in Rome, wasn't it?'

I made no reply, but waited for the next reel. I watched keenly so as to be ready to stop it at once. I knew there would be Sabeth aboard ship, Sabeth playing ping-pong on the promenade deck (with her friend with the toothbrush moustache) and Sabeth in her bikini, Sabeth sticking her tongue out at me when she realized I was filming her – this must all be in the first reel that began with Ivy; so we put that aside. But there were another six or seven reels lying on the table and suddenly, as was only to be expected, there she is – as large as life – Sabeth on the screen. In colour.

I stood up.

Sabeth in Avignon.

But I didn't stop the film, I let the whole reel run through, although the operator told me several times that it couldn't be Guatemala.

I can still see that film.

Her face that will never exist again.

Sabeth in the mistral, she is walking into the wind, the terrace, the Jardin des Papes, everything is fluttering, her hair, her skirt like a balloon, Sabeth by the balustrade, waving.

Her movements.

Sabeth feeding pigeons.

Her laughter, but silent.

The Pont d'Avignon, the old bridge that breaks off in the middle. Sabeth is showing me something, the face she makes when she notices that I am taking a film instead of looking where she is pointing, the way she wrinkles her forehead between the brows, she is saying something.

Landscapes.

The water of the Rhône, cold, Sabeth tries it with her toe and shakes her head; evening sunshine, my long shadow shows on the film.

Her body that no longer exists.

The Roman amphitheatre at Nîmes.

Breakfast under plane trees, the waiter bringing us a second basket of brioches, Sabeth chatting to the waiter, Sabeth looking at me, she fills my cup with black coffee.

Her eyes that no longer exist.

The Pont du Gard.

Sabeth buying postcards to send to Mamma; Sabeth in her black jeans, not knowing I am filming her; Sabeth tossing back her pony-tail.

The Hôtel Henri IV.

Sabeth is sitting on the low window seat, her legs crossed, barefoot, eating cherries, looking down into the street below and spitting out the stones, it is raining.

Her lips . . .

Sabeth talking to a French mule, which, in her opinion, is too heavily loaded.

Her hands . . .

Our Citroën, Model 57.

Her hands, that no longer exist anywhere, she is stroking the mule, her arms, that no longer exist anywhere.

Bullfighting at Arles.

Sabeth combing her hair, a hair-slide between her young

teeth, once more she realizes I am filming her and takes the
slide out of her mouth so as to say something to me, she is
probably telling me to stop filming her, suddenly she can't
help laughing.

Her healthy teeth ...

Her laugh that I shall never hear again.

Her young forehead.

A procession (also in Arles, I think), Sabeth is craning her
neck and smoking with eyes narrowed because of the smoke,
her hands in her trouser pockets. Sabeth standing on a plinth
to see over the heads of the crowd. Baldachins, probably the
sound of bells, but inaudible, the Mother of God, the choir
boys singing, but inaudible.

An avenue in Provence, an avenue of plane trees.

Our picnic by the roadside. Sabeth drinking wine. She has
difficulty in drinking out of the bottle, she closes her eyes and
tries again, then she wipes her mouth, she can't manage it,
she hands the bottle back to me with a shrug of the shoulders.

Pine trees in the mistral.

Her walk ...

Sabeth goes over to a kiosk to buy cigarettes. Sabeth walking. Sabeth, in her usual black jeans, she stands on the edge of
the pavement looking to the left and right, her pony-tail
swings as she turns her head, then she crosses the street diag-
onally towards me.

Her springy walk.

More pines in the mistral.

Sabeth asleep, her mouth half open, a child's mouth, her
loose hair, her seriousness, her closed eyes.

Her face, her face ...

Her breathing body ...

Marseilles. Bulls being shipped in the port, the brown bulls
are led on to the outspread net, then it is drawn up, their
terror, the way they suddenly lose consciousness as they

hang in mid-air, their four legs sticking out through the meshes of the great net, their epileptic-looking eyes.

Pines, in the mistral; again.

L'Unité d'Habitation (Corbusier).

By and large, the lighting of this film is not bad, anyhow it's better than the reels of Guatemala; the colours have turned out superb, I'm amazed.

Sabeth picking flowers.

This time (at last!) I have waved the camera about less, hence the movements of the objects come out much more distinctly.

Surf.

Her fingers, Sabeth sees a cork oak for the first time, her fingers breaking the bark, then she throws it at me!

(A defect in the film.)

Surf at noonday, nothing else.

Sabeth combing her hair again, it's wet, her head is tilted back as she combs, she doesn't see that I am filming her and talks to me while she combs, her hair is darker than usual because it's wet, more chestnut, her green comb is evidently full of sand, she cleans it, her marble skin with drops of water glistening on it, she is still talking to me.

Submarines at Toulon.

The young tramp with the lobster that moves. Sabeth is frightened when the lobster moves.

Our little hotel at Le Trayaz.

Sabeth sitting on a jetty.

More surf.

(Much too long!)

Sabeth out on the jetty again, this time she is standing, our dead daughter, and singing, her hands in her trouser pockets once more, she imagines she is absolutely alone and sings, but inaudibly.

End of the reel.

*

I don't know what the young technician thought and said about me when the gentlemen arrived; I was sitting in the dining car (the Helvetia Express or the Schauinsland Express, I can't remember which now) drinking Steinhäger. I can scarcely remember how I left the Hencke-Bosch building either; without an explanation and without an excuse, I just got up and walked out.

Only I left the films behind.

I told the young technician I had to go and thanked him for his help. I went into the antechamber, where I had left my hat and coat, and asked the young lady for my briefcase, which was still in the directors' office. I was already standing by the lift; it was 11.32 and everyone was ready for the performance, when I asked them to excuse me because I was suffering from pains in the stomach (which wasn't true at all) and got into the lift. They wanted to take me back to my hotel by car, or to hospital; but I hadn't pains in the stomach really. I thanked them and went on foot. Without haste, with no idea where to go to; I didn't know what present-day Düsseldorf looked like, I walked through the city with traffic bumper to bumper, disregarding the traffic lights, I believe, as though blind. I went to the booking-office and bought a ticket, then I boarded the first train out. I sat in the dining-car drinking Steinhäger and looking out of the window, I wasn't crying, I just didn't want to be there, I didn't want to be anywhere. What was the use of looking out of the window? There was nothing for me to see. Her two hands, that no longer existed anywhere, her movements as she tossed the pony-tail towards the back of her head or combed her hair, her teeth, her lips, her eyes that no longer existed anywhere, her forehead – where could I look for them? All I wished was that I had never existed. What was the use of returning to Zurich? What was the use of going to Athens? I sat in the dining car thinking. Why not take these two forks, hold them upright in my hands and let my head fall, so as to get rid of my eyes?

My operation has been fixed for tomorrow.

PS.
All the time I was travelling I had no idea what Hanna did after the calamity. Not a single letter from Hanna. Even now I don't know. When I ask her, all she replies is 'What can I do?' I no longer understand anything. How can Hanna stand me, after all that has happened? She comes here and goes away and comes back, she brings me anything I need, she listens to me. What does she think? Her hair has grown whiter. Why doesn't she tell me I have ruined her life? I can't picture her life after all that has happened. For one moment alone I understood Hanna – when she hammered my face with her fists beside the deathbed. Since then I have never understood her.

16 July. Zurich.
I believe that I travelled from Düsseldorf to Zurich merely because I hadn't seen my native city for several decades.

There was nothing for me to do in Zurich.

Williams was expecting me in Paris.

In Zurich, when he drew up alongside me and stepped out of his car to greet me, I once more failed to recognize him; just like the last time – a skull with skin stretched over it, the skin like yellowish leather, his balloon-like tummy, his protruding ears, his cordiality, his death's head laugh, his eyes still alive but sunken. I only knew that I knew him, but for the first moment I didn't know who he was.

'Always in a hurry,' he laughed, 'always in a hurry.'

What was I doing in Zurich?

'You don't recognize me again?' he asked.

He looked ghastly, I didn't know what to say, of course I recognized him, it was only the initial shock and then the fear that I might put my foot in it. I said:

'Of course I have time.'

Then we went together to the Café Odéon.

'I'm sorry I didn't recognize you that time in Paris,' I said.

He bore no ill will, he laughed, I listened, my eyes on his old teeth, it only looked as though he was laughing, his teeth were far too large, his muscles were no longer strong enough for a face that wasn't laughing, it was a conversation with a death's head, I had to pull myself together to prevent myself from asking Professor O. when he was going to die. He laughed:

'What's that you're drawing, Faber?'

I was drawing on the little marble table, that was all, a spiral, there was a fossilized snail in the yellow marble, hence my spiral – I put my propelling pencil away and we discussed the world situation, his laughter disturbed me so much that I simply couldn't think of anything to say.

I wasn't very talkative, he remarked.

One of the Odéon waiters, Peter, an old Viennese, still recognized me; he thought I hadn't changed.

Professor O. laughed.

He thought it a pity I hadn't delivered my dissertation (on the so-called Maxwell's demon) before I left Zurich.

The Odéon tarts were just the same as ever.

'Didn't you know,' he laughed, 'that they are going to pull down the Odéon?'

All of a sudden he asked:

'How's your lovely daughter?'

He had seen Sabeth as we said good-bye in the café after meeting in Paris – 'the other day, in Paris', as he put it. That was the afternoon before Sabeth and I went to the Opéra, the eve of our honeymoon. All I said was:

'How did you know she was my daughter?'

'I just thought so!'

He laughed as he said it.

I had no reason for being in Zurich, that same day (after my chat in the Odéon with Professor O.) I went out to Kloten to complete my journey by plane.

My last flight!

Another Super-Constellation.

It was really a smooth flight, the foehn was blowing only gently above the Alps, which I knew to some extent from my youth but had never flown over before, it was a blue afternoon with the usual wall of clouds piled up by the foehn. the Vierwaldstättersee, to the right the Wetterhorn and behind it the Eiger and Jungfrau and possibly the Finsteraahorn, my knowledge of our mountains is a bit rusty these days, I have other things on my mind . . .

What exactly?

Valleys in the slanting light of late afternoon, mountainsides covered in shadow, gorges filled with shadow and streaked by white streams, willows in the slanting light, haystacks red in the sun, a flock in a hollow full of scree beyond the edge of the forest – like white maggots! (Of course Sabeth would have thought of some other comparison, but I don't know what.) My forehead against the cold windowpane filled with idle thoughts . . .

The wish to smell hay.

Never to fly again.

The wish to walk on earth – there beneath the last firs standing in the sunshine, to smell their resin and listen to the water, which is probably roaring, to drink water.

Everything goes past as though in a film.

The wish to grasp the earth.

Instead, we rise higher and higher.

How thin the zone of life really is, a few hundred yards, then the atmosphere already becomes too thin, too cold, it's really an oasis that man inhabits, the green floor of the valley, its narrow branches, then the end of the oasis, it is as though the forests have been cut off (at 6,000 feet in this part of the world, at 12,000 feet in Mexico), for a while there are still flocks and herds grazing at the limits of possible life, flowers – I can't see them, but I know they are there – colourful and sweet-scented, but tiny, insects, then only scree, then snow . . .

Farther on another reservoir.

Its water: like Pernod, greenish and cloudy, the mirror-white of névé upon it, a rowboat against the bank, a multiple-arch dam, not a soul in sight.

Then the first mist, scudding along.

The crevasses – as green as bottle-glass. Sabeth would have said: as emerald! Our twenty-one points game again. The rocks in the evening light – like gold. I think: like amber, because lustreless and almost transparent, or like bone, because pale and brittle. The shadow of our aeroplane on moraines and glaciers; every time it drops down into the chasms it seems to be lost and swallowed up, but a few seconds later it is adhering to the next wall of rock; for the first instant it looks as though it has been laid on with a builder's trowel, it doesn't lie there like a layer of plaster, however, but glides along and drops back into the void on the other side of the ridge. Sabeth would have compared the shadow of our plane to a bat. I can't think of anything and lose a point. I have something else in mind. A trail in the névé, human footprints, it looks like a row of rivets; Sabeth would have compared it to a necklace, bluish, hanging in a wide loop around a white bosom of névé. What I have in mind is this: supposing I were now standing on that peak, what should I do? It would be too late to climb down; dusk is already falling in the valleys and the shades of evening extend over whole glaciers and bend at right angles down the vertical walls. What should I do? We fly past; we can see the cross marking the peak, it gleams white but very lonely, a light the mountaineer never sees, because he has to go down before he reaches it, a light that has to be paid for with death, but very beautiful, for an instant, then clouds, air pockets, the southern face of the Alps covered with clouds, as was to be expected; the clouds are like gypsum, like cauliflower, like foam with tiny bubbles, I don't know what Sabeth would have thought of, they change quickly, every now and then there is a hole in the clouds, and we can see down into the depths – a black wood, a stream, the wood like a hedgehog, but only for a second, the clouds drift into one another, the shadows of the higher clouds fall on those below, shadows like curtains, we fly through the pile of cloud heaped up in the sunlight in front of us – as though our plane were going to smash itself against the cloudbanks, a mountain of steam, but rounded and white like Greek marble, granular.

We fly into it.

Since my forced landing in Tamaulipas I have always sat so that I can see the undercarriage when they lower it, anxious to observe whether the runway at the last minute, when the wheels touch it, does not after all change into a desert.

Milan.

A cable to Hanna announcing my arrival.

Where else could I go?

It is extraordinary how an undercarriage, twin tyres with telescopic suspension and lubricating oil on the shining metal, all as it should be, suddenly acts like a demon when it touches the ground, a demon that suddenly turns the runway into desert – a figment of the imagination which I myself did not take seriously; I have never met a demon in my life, apart from the so-called Maxwell's demon, which, as everyone knows, is not a demon at all.

Rome.

A cable to Williams, giving notice.

I gradually calmed down.

It was night when we continued the flight, and we flew too far north, so that – around midnight – I couldn't make out the Gulf of Corinth.

Everything as usual.

The exhaust sending out a shower of sparks into the darkness.

The flashing green light on the wing.

Moonlight on the wing.

The red glow in the engine-cowl.

I was intensely interested, as though I was flying for the first time in my life; I saw the undercarriage swing slowly out, the searchlights blazed forth from under the wings, projecting their white radiance into the discs of the propellers, then they went out again; there were lights below us, the streets of Athens, or rather Piraeus, we sank down, then the ground-lights, yellow, the runway, our searchlights again, then the customary gentle bump (without any jerk forward into unconsciousness) with the customary clouds of dust rising behind the undercarriage.

I undo my belt.

Hanna at the airport.

I see her through my window.

Hanna in black.

I have only my briefcase, my Baby Hermes, a coat and a hat, so that the customs are quickly dealt with; I am the first out, but I daren't even wave. Just before the barrier I simply stood still (says Hanna) and waited for Hanna to come up to me. This was the first time I had seen Hanna in black. She kissed me on the forehead. She recommended the Hotel Estia Emborron.

Today nothing but tea, the whole examination business all over again, afterwards I felt done in. Tomorrow the operation at last.

Up to the present I have been to her grave only once, since they kept me here straight away (I only asked for an examination); a hot grave, flowers wither in half a day.

6 P.M.
They have taken my Baby Hermes away.

7.30 P.M.
Hanna has been here again.

Midnight.
I haven't slept for a minute and don't want to. I know everything. Tomorrow they are going to open me up and find out what they already know; that there is nothing they can do. They will sew me up and when I come to, they will tell me the operation has been carried out. I shall believe them, although I know everything. I shan't admit that the pains have come back worse than ever. They argue like this: if I knew I had cancer of the stomach I should put a bullet through my brains. I cling to this life as never before, and if it was only another year, a miserable year, a quarter of a year, two months (that would be September and October), I should

hope, although I know I am lost. But I am not alone, Hanna is
my friend, and I am not alone.

2.40 A.M.
Wrote a letter to Hanna.

4.00 A.M.
Arrangements in case of death; all written evidence such as
reports, letters, loose-leaf notebooks, are to be destroyed, none
of it is true. To be alive: to be in the light. Driving donkeys
around somewhere (like that old man in Corinth) – that's all
our job amounts to! The main thing is to stand up to the
light, to joy (like our child) in the knowledge that I shall be
extinguished in the light over gorse, asphalt and sea, to stand
up to time, or rather to eternity in the instant. To be eternal
means to have existed.

4.15 A.M.
Hanna too no longer has a home, she only told me today
(yesterday!). She is now living in a boarding house. My cable
from Caracas didn't even reach her. It must have been around
this time that Hanna embarked on a ship. Her first idea was
to spend a year on the islands, where she has Greek acquaint-
ances from the time of the excavations (Delos); living is supposed to be very cheap in the islands. In Mykonos you can
buy a house for two hundred dollars, thinks Hanna, in
Amorgos for one hundred dollars. She is not working at the
Institute any more, as I have been thinking all the time.
Hanna tried to let her flat with the contents, but was unable
to do so quickly enough; so she sold everything and gave
away many of her books. She simply couldn't stand it in
Athens any longer, she said. When she went aboard ship she
thought of Paris, perhaps also of London; the future was
altogether uncertain, for it's not so easy, thinks Hanna, to
find a new job at her age, as a secretary, for instance, Hanna

never thought for a moment of asking me for help; that's why she didn't write to me. Fundamentally, Hanna had only one aim: to get away from Greece. She left the city without saying good-bye to her friends here, apart from the director of the Institute, whom she greatly esteems. She spent the last hours before her departure out by the grave; she had to be on board by 2 P.M. sailing at 3 P.M., but for some reason sailing was delayed almost an hour. All of a sudden (says Hanna) it struck her as senseless and she left the ship with her hand luggage. For the three big trunks in the hold, it was too late; the trunks sailed on to Naples and are expected back shortly. At first she lived in the Hotel Estia Emborron, but this was too expensive for her in the long run; she called back at the Institute, where her former assistant had meanwhile taken over her job with a three-year contract; this could not be altered now, because her successor had waited long enough and had no intention of voluntarily returning to his old job. The director was apparently very nice about it all, but the Institute hadn't the money to employ two people for one job. All they could give her was the prospect of occasional free-lance work and recommendations abroad. But Hanna wasn't to stay in Athens. I don't know whether Hanna expected me here or whether she wanted to leave Athens so as not to see me again. It was pure chance that she received my cable from Rome in time; when it arrived, she just happened to have come to the empty flat to give the key to the caretaker. Hanna's present job consists in conducting visitors round the museum in the morning, the Acropolis in the afternoon and Sounion in the evening. In particular she conducts parties that do everything in one day, organized by Mediterranean travel agencies.

6 A.M.

Wrote another letter to Hanna.

6.45 A.M.

I don't know why Joachim hanged himself; Hanna keeps asking me. How should I know? She keeps coming back to it, although I know less about Joachim than Hanna does. She says: 'When the child was there, she never reminded me of you, she was my child, mine alone.' With reference to Joachim: 'I loved him just because he was not the father of my child, and during the first few years everything was so simple.' Hanna thinks our child would never have been born if we hadn't parted when we did. Hanna is convinced of this. Hanna made up her mind before I even reached Baghdad, apparently; she wanted a child, the whole thing took her by surprise, and only when I had disappeared did she discover that she wanted a child (says Hanna) without a father, not our child, but her child. She was alone and happy to be pregnant, and when she went to Joachim to let herself be talked round, Hanna had already made up her mind to have the child; she didn't mind Joachim thinking he had led her to reach a crucial decision in her life, nor his falling in love with her, which soon afterwards led to marriage. My unfortunate remark in her flat earlier on, 'You're behaving like a hen,' made a considerable impression on Hanna, because, as she confessed, Joachim once used exactly the same words, Joachim provided for the child without interfering in its upbringing; it wasn't his child, nor mine either, it was a fatherless child, hers and hers alone, a child that did not concern any man, which suited Joachim all right, at least during the earliest years, as long as it was a baby, which in any case belongs to the mother, and Joachim welcomed it because it made Hanna happy. My name was never mentioned, says Hanna. Joachim had no reason to feel jealous, and he wasn't jealous so far as I was concerned; he saw that I wasn't the

216

father in the eyes of the world, which didn't know anything about it, and most certainly not in the eyes of Hanna, who simply forgot me (as Hanna repeatedly assures me) without any reproach. Things became more difficult between Joachim and Hanna when questions of upbringing arose more frequently: less because of differences of opinion, which were few, than because Joachim simply couldn't bear the way Hanna considered herself, in everything related to children, the one and only authority. Hanna admitted that Joachim was easy to get on with, allergic only in this one respect.

He evidently hoped more and more for a child, a child of theirs, which would give him the status of a father; he thought that then everything would fall into place; Elsbeth considered him her Papa; she loved him, but Joachim distrusted her, says Hanna, and felt himself superfluous. There were all sorts of sensible reasons for not bringing any more children into the world, especially for a German half-Jewess; Hanna still keeps insisting on these reasons, as though I disputed them. Joachim didn't believe her reasons. His suspicion: 'You don't want a father in the home!' He thought Hanna only wanted children if the father afterwards disappeared. One thing I didn't know: Joachim had been making plans to emigrate since 1935; he was determined not to let anything part him from Hanna. Hanna never thought of separation either; she wanted to go with Joachim to Canada or Australia, she trained as laboratory assistant, so that she could help him in whatever part of the world he went to. But it never got that far. When Joachim learned that Hanna had had herself sterilized he took the drastic step of volunteering for the Wehrmacht (although to the annoyance of his clan, he had been able to claim exemption). Hanna has never forgotten him. Although she did not live without men during the ensuing years, she sacrificed her whole life to her child. She worked in Paris, later in London, East Berlin, Athens. She fled with her child. Where there was no German-language school, she taught her child herself and, at the age of forty, took up the violin again, so that she could accompany her child. Nothing was too much for Hanna, where the child was concerned. She cared for her child in a cellar, when the Wehrmacht came to Paris, and ventured out in the street to fetch medicines. Hanna didn't spoil her child; Hanna is too intelligent for that, to my mind, even if (during the last few days) she keeps on describing herself as an idiot. Why did I say that? She keeps asking. Why did I say 'Your child', instead of 'Our child'? Was I reproaching her or was the expression merely prompted by cowardice? I don't understand her question. Did I realize at the time how right I was? And why did I say the other day: 'You're behaving like a hen?' I have withdrawn and recanted this remark several times, now that I know all that Hanna has done; but it is Hanna who can't forget it. Can I forgive her?! She wept, she went down on her knees, when the deaconess might have come in at any moment, when Hanna kissed my hand I could no longer recognize her. All I can understand is why, after everything that has happened, Hanna will never leave Athens, never leave the grave of our child. We shall both remain here, I think. I can understand, too, why she gave up her flat with the empty rooms; Hanna found it hard enough to let the girl go away by herself, if only for half a year. Hanna always knew her child would leave her one day; but even Hanna could not foresee that on this journey Sabeth would meet her father, who would destroy everything . . .

8.45 A.M.
    They're coming.

My work on this book was assisted by a grant from the Pro-Helvetia foundation. I wish to conclude it by expressing my thanks to this foundation for its aid.

M. F.

Zurich, August 1957

More About Penguins
and Pelicans

For further information about books available from Penguins please write to Dept EP, Penguin Books Ltd, Harmondsworth, Middlesex UB7 0DA.

In the U.S.A.: For a complete list of books available from Penguins in the United States write to Dept CS, Penguin Books, 625 Madison Avenue, New York, New York 10022.

In Canada: For a complete list of books available from Penguins in Canada write to Penguin Books Canada Ltd, 2801 John Street, Markham, Ontario L3R 1B4.

In Australia: For a complete list of books available from Penguins in Australia write to the Marketing Department, Penguin Books Australia Ltd, P.O. Box 257, Ringwood, Victoria 3134.

In New Zealand: For a complete list of books available from Penguins in New Zealand write to the Marketing Department, Penguin Books (N.Z.) Ltd, P.O. Box 4019, Auckland 10.

Also by Max Frisch

I'm Not Stiller

'Every word is false and true, that is the nature of words'

So how can we ever know for certain the identity of the man in the cell? He claims to be an American citizen named White but the police are unshakable in their belief that he is Anatol Ludwig Stiller, the Swiss sculptor who vanished nearly a decade before. Despite the insistence of Stiller's wife, brother and mistress, and in the face of every incentive to admit that he *is* Stiller, the man perseveres in his denial. Yet he betrays uncanny perceptions of the personality he disclaims – sculptor, husband, lover . . . prisoner.

I'm Not Stiller reveals the comic and disturbing literary powers of Max Frisch as he explores the nature of identity.

'The comparison with Thomas Mann can be soberly made' – *Encounter*

A House and Its Head
Ivy Compton-Burnett

In 1935 a reviewer wrote of *A House and Its Head*, 'It is as if one's next door neighbour leaned over the garden wall, and remarked, in the same breath and chatty tone, that he had mown the lawn in the morning and thrust his wife's head in the gas-oven after lunch.' Here, through stark dialogue and a finely integrated plot, Ivy Compton-Burnett writes about an upper-class Victorian family, piercing the façade of conventionality to reveal the human capacity for evil . . .

The Story of the Eye
Georges Bataille

Widely regarded as the greatest sexual/pornographic novel of this century, *The Story of the Eye* was first published in 1928, and in it Bataille explores his own sexual obsessions.

This edition also includes Susan Sontag's essay, 'The Pornographic Imagination', which discusses this and other erotic classics, together with Roland Barthes's essay on *The Story of the Eye*.

A Life
Italo Svevo

First published in 1893, *Una Vita* and its author remained in obscurity for over thirty years until James Joyce hailed Svevo as a major literary discovery. As in all his works, Svevo is concerned here with the bourgeois soul, and its inability to will or act. His heroes are typically men of business, but with cultural pretentions and he depicts them in their free time when they are not working. It is less important to Svevo whether they have spare money or not: the important thing is that they always have time to spare. How they lose it, use it or kill it forms his major theme – worked with all the quixotic genius of which he was capable.